EDITIONS LTD

MEAT EATERS & PLANT EATERS

T0163987

Meat Eaters
& Plant Eaters

stories by
JESSICA TREAT

AMERICAN READER SERIES, NO. 11

BOA EDITIONS, LTD. ~ ROCHESTER, NY ~ 2009

For information about permission to reuse any material from this book
please contact The Permissions Company at www.permissionscompany.
com or e-mail permdude@eclipse.net.

Publications by BOA Editions, Ltd.—a not-for-profit corporation under
section 501 (c) (3) of the United States Internal Revenue Code—are made
possible with funds from a variety of sources, including public funds from
the New York State Council on the Arts, a state agency; the Literature Pro-
gram of the National Endowment for the Arts; the County of Monroe, NY;
the Lannan Foundation for support of the Lannan Translations Selection
Series; the Sonia Raiziss Giop Charitable Foundation; the Mary S. Mulligan
Charitable Trust; the Rochester Area Community Foundation; the Arts &
Cultural Council for Greater Rochester; the Steeple-Jack Fund; the Ames-
Amzalak Memorial Trust in memory of Henry Ames, Semon Amzalak and
Dan Amzalak; and contributions from many individuals nationwide. See
Colophon on page 160 for special individual acknowledgments.

Cover Design: Sandy Knight
Interior Design and Composition: Richard Foerster
BOA Logo: Mirko

Library of Congress Cataloging-in-Publication Data

Treat, Jessica, 1958–
  Meat eaters & plant eaters : stories / by Jessica Treat.
     p. cm. — (American reader series ; no. 11)
  ISBN 1-934414-22-0 (alk. paper)
  I. Title. II. Title: Meat eaters and plant eaters.

  PS3570.R359M43 2009
  813'.54—dc22

                         2009001762

BOA Editions, Ltd.
A. Poulin, Jr., Founder (1938–1996)
250 North Goodman Street, Suite 306
Rochester, NY 14607
www.boaeditions.org

NATIONAL
ENDOWMENT
FOR THE ARTS

A great nation
deserves great art.

State of the Arts

NYSCA

Contents

I
Drive

II
Meat Eaters & Plant Eaters

III
Close Your Eyes

IV
Little Bitches

To my family:
my mother, Sharon; Roger; Carolyn; Rory;
my son, Kai; and to the memory of my father,
with love and gratitude.

I
Drive

Beached

She's taken the car he doesn't know where. She's gone off again. No, they don't have another car. No, he cannot say where and no, he does not think she will call, write a note retrospectively . . .

Why does she have to do this? Why is it so difficult to write out on a scrap of paper, tape it to the door: I've gone to _____. I'll be back by _____. Surely one can be spontaneous, feel free, but also keep one's partner informed. No, not possible. Quite impossible for her.

He makes himself a cup of coffee. Strong as he likes it, no milk or sugar. For all he knows, she's gone off to get herself a cappuccino somewhere. As if coffee tastes better in a public place than home-brewed in their kitchen.

There was that time they'd stopped at a local favorite for lunch—they were on vacation, a small town
in New Brunswick—a lovely screen porch, tables with
vases of flowers, but no, she chose the indoor part of
the restaurant. He'd relented. But felt the need to ask:
Why, on a beautiful summer day—?

She shrugged. "There are more people here."

Exactly. Just the reason for getting away.

Like when they'd arrive at the beach together, he'd
immediately head down to the end, where few people
sat, where a slow rivulet of water trickled down the
rocks. But he could feel her at his side, not quite with
him—tugging invisibly—in the other direction.

"What?" he asked.

"I thought we might sit over there, where the other
people are—"

Is it a fatal flaw? That she is drawn to people and
places, while he is pulled toward the removed, remote,
the private, and—it seems to him—infinitely more
beautiful.

It occurs to him that this is exactly what draws
him to her: her own remoteness. "Other people I know
might be bothered," he remembers telling her, early
on in their relationship, a hike they'd taken somewhere—"by the fact that you go for such long periods
without saying anything. It might unnerve them. It
doesn't bother me though. I feel comfortable with that
about you."

Yet he also saw she could be with others: a certain volubility welled up inside her, a cascade of words—ones he hadn't been treated to in a good long while.

He wants to get in the car to drive to find her. Then remembers that she has it. The car.

He stands at the door, thinking he hears the rumble of its engine, far off, getting closer—

But no, it's nothing. A lawn mower or tractor working its slow progress toward him.

In Summer

The handle turned, and with a push, the door opened. The floorboards were bare under her feet, the room, empty—but for dust and cobwebs, the scurrying, almost transparent spiders. She found a bird nest in a corner, bits of plastic woven in with long pine needles and small twigs. There was nothing else but a wooden spool, its lavender thread nearly faded to grey. The bird nest felt light in her hand, fragile yet sturdy. Birds were expert builders. She realized in her hand she held another empty room.

There were stairs. She climbed them, found other rooms, small with low ceilings—as in so many old houses—large enough for a bed, maybe a four-poster, as if all they were ever designed for was sleeping. She felt vaguely guilty; she was acting as she had as a young girl, searching, exploring, opening doors that were meant to remain closed. Her husband and child felt faraway; they were napping in the summerhouse they'd rented down the road.

Five rooms with doors facing the stairway. There was only one she hadn't entered. She turned the handle, but it wouldn't open. She tried again. The door was locked. If only she could see in . . . but even the keyhole was too small to be looked through. She felt the top of the doorframe for a key; a layer of dust greeted her fingertips. Again she felt the barrenness of the house, its quiet stillness, of its being swept clean of secrets.

But for this one. Perhaps the locked door led nowhere. Perhaps what lay on the other side was another empty room, locked not to keep anything in or out, but only by accident. What lay on the other side would always be disappointing, would never be as she imagined: plush chairs covered with purple velvet, velvet drapes and scattered pillows. A wall of old photographs: a woman with beaklike nose, severe in her hair bun, a child in falling-down stockings and starched white dress standing in front of a rose bush. An orchard behind her, the smell of summer apples, a path leading to a house . . . a house just like this one.

She made her way down the stairs, closed the front door behind her. She walked quickly along the road, thinking of her husband and child, surely awake now. She looked down at the bird nest she still held, spool of thread nestled inside. The air smelled of apples.

A Visit

The telephone rang while he was running the vacuum cleaner. He didn't know this until later—so loud was the noise of the Electrolux and so concentrated was he on the task at hand: getting the cat's fur off the carpet, the bits and twigs and leaves dragged from outside, the ash from cigarettes. He needed it to look good when she arrived; he needed to feel everything was in order for the evening to proceed well: the house clean, dishes done, leaves raked outside. She would arrive and they would talk, as they did the last time, sitting side by side on the couch. He'd offer her tea and figs, later he'd make dinner and then she would or wouldn't spend the night. She hadn't yet done that. He would see if he wanted her to. He hadn't yet. Wanted her to. That could change of course. He knew that.

There was a picture of him as a child—a black-and-white photograph in a small frame. He was burying his dog in the sand at the beach; only the small dog's head emerged from a mound. He was smiling. He looked happy, absorbed. He hadn't had a happy childhood—he'd told her that. With his brothers so much older, he might as well have been an only child. But he looked pleased in the photograph, smiling for the camera, proud of his job with the dog.

"Did you love going to the beach as a child?" she asked. She knew she did—loved the sand, the waves, the feeling of summer stretching out—like the ocean itself—so vast one felt insignificant. She liked that sense—of being only a speck in the universe—it was comforting somehow.

"I didn't like it at all."

"What?" She hadn't been prepared for that. She thought she hadn't heard him. "What?" she asked—a bad habit, her husband always told her, *You heard me perfectly well, I'm not going to repeat anything.* "What?" she said, unable to undo her bad habits, even with him.

"I didn't like going to the beach at all. I still don't. I'd see all those people there on the sand in their half-nakedness. All those bodies . . . and I was afraid of the water. I never learned to swim very well. I thought I'd drown. I found it so uncomfortable: the sun, the sand, the seaweed, and the people with their rolls of flab, those skimpy suits . . ."

She stared at him. Why was he telling her this? She felt a tightness in her chest, a tightly wrapped pall of panic. It was unraveling itself; she felt it spreading through her. He was going on—bodies in bathing suits . . . fear of drowning . . . shellfish . . . lobster . . .

She felt herself sinking away from him, tried to hold on, to dissipate the feeling in her chest: We will never sleep together. He is telling me that now. . . . We will never lie next to one another without our clothes on. . . . She tried hard to swim up to the surface, to find what she could tell him—"But . . . the ocean, didn't you love to listen to the sound of the waves?" Had he never slept beneath the stars? On a sandy beach somewhere? They would never have an affair . . . and she'd been prepared. She loved him—

"I hate lobster. Can't eat mussels, all that shellfish . . ."

He had stood up, he would prepare dinner for her—pasta with vegetables—it was what he made—a version of what he'd made the last time, the other times as well. True, he had never visited her . . . But how could he? She lived with her husband . . . He, on the other hand, had been divorced for three years.

"Do you have any more pictures? Any others?" she asked.

~

Trail

Then she heard the dog bark. Strange since there had been no car on the road, no sound of steps. Of course the snow was freshly fallen, soft and plush, to muffle any sound. He barked again. Was it a stray cat? Or coon? Deer most likely.

She stepped out onto the porch. The air felt crisp, chill. "Tigre, what do you hear? What do you smell? Hmm?" and scratched him behind the ear. His tail wagged for her, but he kept his eye on the road, ears back, and barked again. She tried to see what he did—what scent was he picking up on? Or sound? The breeze was light, and the moon slipped behind clouds then reappeared—or rather, it must be the clouds that moved. Tigre was in the driveway now barking frantically.

"*Que pasa? Que pasa, Tigre, eh?*" As if he'd be able to answer her better if she spoke in Spanish. She walked to the end of the driveway—not a long walk at all—50 feet? She was no good at judging distances—still in sight of the house, the road. She felt cold now, not having stopped to put on a jacket before venturing outside. She hugged herself as she walked, trying to retain warmth.

There was nothing to find. Nor did she notice any footsteps in the snow other than Tigre's and her own, the tire tracks of her Forester.

"C'mon, Tigre, let's go—," and he came reluctantly behind her, his magnetic sense of smell clearly still pulling him elsewhere.

The house was locked. She must not have undone the bolt, it must have locked behind her. And she did not have keys. There was of course the other door. She walked to the back to try it, but no—it was locked also.

She tried to think clearly: the car, her Forester? But the keys were in the house. Her cell? No—she'd brought it inside to recharge it. The neighbors—she'd have to walk to the neighbors.

It was hard not to stop the voice of blame: *Idiot! Idiota! Walking out, what were you thinking? Not even grabbing a sweater!* She'd felt so warm and cozy inside . . . no she wouldn't blame Tigre; it was not his fault she could not think ahead.

Trail

The Kramers, a half mile down the road, were not home. She knocked, looked in windows—nothing. She didn't know them well; they hadn't been overly friendly when she'd moved in, but surely they'd begun to warm up a little—Hilda, her husband Jonathan—through socializing? *SHIT*, she cried, stamping her feet in the snow, *SHIT SHIT SHIT*. Her eyes smarted, she was so angry. Tigre wagged his tail as if he knew, licked her ungloved hand. He seemed to be trying to cheer her. "What do we do now?" she asked. She calculated. They should try the other direction, the Van Burens—perhaps they'd be home. They were closer than the house past the Kramers—besides she wanted to walk past her house again. There must be something else to do, a window to try? Or break? Some other way to get inside what seemed like nirvana now.

It's the end of the world as we know it, it's the end of the world as we know it and I feel fine . . . REM's song ran through her head, an endless loop (was she trying to convince herself?). In reality, her teeth were chattering.

What had made her think she could live alone? With no one but a dog for company? Was she crazy? *Such a fuck-up. Such a goddamn fuck-up.*

An hour later, inside (the locksmith gone now), she had calculated her losses: her laptop computer, the CD player, her jewelry, her wallet even.

Gone. The police were on their way. Would there be finger printing? No. Whoever it was—much too canny for that. No trail but her own.

She leaned back into the couch and closed her eyes. She felt Tigre beside her, curling into her, nosing the hand she rested on her kneecap.

"Gone," she said aloud, "Stolen . . ." And saying the words aloud, she suddenly knew who it was who'd taken them. Her ex. It was him, she knew. Her heart raced. *What to do?* The police were coming, she reminded herself. Why did she feel he was there in the house? Watching and waiting? From where was she getting this X-ray vision? This keen sense of sound? Of smell?

"Tigre," she said, "Tigre . . ." He nudged his nose into her, not noticing anything it seemed but the comfort of her smell.

Listing

He read the note, folded it, tucked it in his pocket. He'd found it by the roadside. He'd hoped for something more interesting, not:

> *lemons*
> *dish detergent*
> *butter*
> *scones*

The handwriting was old-fashioned, an old lady's, limp and loose; one could see the well-formed characters but they'd lost definition, the hand a bit shaky.

He'd been hoping for something more revealing, revelatory, a sign or portent:

Meet me at the boathouse at 2:00 P.M.

Or:

You will soon receive an unexpected visitor.

He thought no more about it. Just a shopping list—someone else's unmet needs. What were his own? What would his list look like?

> *a love relationship*
> *a more rewarding job*
> *a goal and destination . . .*

He hadn't always been so without definition. His figure had once cut a sharper shape. He hadn't always had his father's ailing health to look after . . .

The smell of pine sap reached him. He was walking past the park where he and Elena had first met, she with her little dog—Clemence, she called it—which seemed to him too much of a person's name. But then Elena and Clemence were awfully bonded, and that was the problem, wasn't it—it left no room for him—how, after all, does one compete with a cute little fluff ball of fur? Something that promised loyalty, fun and affection, yet never really demanded anything—just some food and caressing—a minimum of fuss.

Of course, Elena thought him crazy—jealous of a Yorkshire Terrier. But he was. She couldn't see that her devotion was extreme, her attachment unhealthy. Instead it was: "You're the one with the problem! Unable to attach yourself to anyone!"

There was perhaps some truth to the statement, he could admit, which showed finally that he was much more reasonable than she—who could admit nothing, nothing was ever wrong with her or Clemence—how quickly she flew to her dog's defense! "She doesn't shed, what are you talking about?" "She does not eat too much!" "She doesn't smell—what's the matter with you?"

It was all his problem then. His obsessing over a dog. Poor Clemence. It's true he'd thought of killing it. He'd sometimes wanted to. But the thought of the after-math—Elena mad with grief and rage—was not a happy picture. It wouldn't make her run to him, he knew. She'd just burrow further into her devotion and commitment, if only to the memory of Clemence.

Was it too difficult to form a new attachment at age 48? We've lived too long, he thought. Loved enough, or not enough, but have enough of our identities intact that the need for someone else just isn't strong enough. And yet . . . The last time he saw her he'd wanted her with a ferocity that surprised him. Her smile, the way her hair fell in wisps around her ears, her legs—still shapely and attractive beneath her short skirt. She was kind and funny and physically attractive, and having been in a number of relationships over the years, from two days to 14 years, he knew this was all that mattered to him now, it had boiled down to this: thoughtfulness, a sense of humor, an attractive physique. But sans Clemence. Just get rid of the dog.

He'd wandered onto the trail that began in the park and wound its way through the woods. He trod the path without thinking, without noticing: faint sound of birds, insects, twigs crackling. Soon the sun would be sinking. He thought of the list he'd pocketed:

> *lemons*
> *dish detergent*
> *butter*
> *scones*

He could remember the items easily. And if he placed those four items in his shopping basket? Would he have the answer? How simple, really, so simple. His step quickened. He knew the Quick Mart would be open now; the trail led almost to its doorstep. He smiled—at nothing, to no one in particular.

Drive

He stepped out of nowhere. You hadn't seen him walking, hadn't seen him at all, but suddenly he was there, running across the road. You hit the brakes hard. You've hit him, you think, see his body bumping up onto your hood, his face shattering the windshield—your secret terror: to kill someone while driving. But the windshield does not shatter. You've only bumped him.

You roll down the window to yell at him or apologize—you don't know which—you're frustrated and flabbergasted, "What the hell do you think you're doing?"

"Could you give me a lift to Bainbridge?" he says in his scruffy British accent. He wants a ride. It's his technique, you realize, for getting one. Stopping a car in midstream—and because he's caught you off guard, "Go ahead, get in."

You can't say anything, still shaking some—you almost killed him—how about it then? Was it your fault? And know it wasn't, but know also that if he'd died, you'd have lived with the guilt for years—regardless. But he interrupts. You hadn't wanted to be reminded: someone else is in the car with you. You like your solitude and besides you know your car smells: sour milk from spilled coffee, perspiration mixed with something like soy sauce—it's your private space and whatever made you let someone in? But you almost killed him. That's enough, isn't it, to shake off habit, that covering you always wear—that's enough, isn't it?

"You aren't from here, are you?" he says.

You avoid answering him, counter with a question, "What about you?" but realize it sounds like tacit consent, no I'm not, what about you? Well it's none of his business—why should you tell him that you summer here and have for years? You owe him nothing since his life was spared. But he's still sitting there, expectant. You realize he hasn't answered your question. Did you even ask it? You begin to wonder.

"Mind if I smoke?"

"Go ahead," you say for the second time, wonder what's made you so compliant, realize it must be his accent, scruffy British and charming.

When he offers you one of his hand-rolled cigarettes you take one, start to believe it must have been fated, your bumping into this stranger from out of nowhere and that sort of thinking, "magical thinking," a shrink would tell you, is only the second of many mistakes you'll make that evening.

Teacup

The cup was discovered under the table. No one remembered putting it there—nor using it, for that matter: it was dainty, a pale pink pattern, unlike any of their dishes—who could have left it?

Of course when they'd moved in, the house was empty. A few rolls of shelving paper in the linen closet, an air freshener—unopened—in the bathroom cabinet (she threw it out, she hated its false fragrance)—nothing more. Yet now a strange cup sat under the table . . . how did it get there?

She made a mental list of the visitors they'd entertained in the past few months—there weren't many—June Hedges, Branford and his wife Sara, Tilly and her son Matthew—could they have brought it? But it was so unlike the cup of a child. It was more like the cup your grandmother or your Aunt Tabitha in England would have used. . . .

She got on her hands and knees, crouching to look under the space of the table. Was there a dark corner it could have rolled from, somewhere she'd never before noticed? But no: it was relatively clean—save for a few spots from spilled coffee, some balls of dust and a plastic twisty.

Now she held the cup in her two hands. She brought it to her mouth as if to drink but instead sniffed it. What did it smell of? Jasmine or rose water? She tried to discern but she had no perfumer's nose . . . decided finally it smelled of nothing but porcelain.

She placed it on the top shelf of the open cupboard. She wanted to be able to see it, to fix on it daily. It was a mystery she would live with.

Covered Bridge

I decide to visit the bridge. Of course it's not the same one. It's been reconstructed, painted a slate-grey. I haven't come here since the driving trip a friend and I took almost 14 years ago. How odd that I should not revisit it until now.

We had next to no money, just enough in fact to pay for the car we rented. We drove from Brooklyn, where we lived, all the way to the Adirondacks. We put 1,000 miles on the car. We made few stops: at cemeteries for walks, at diners where we filled up on breakfast.

We drove back on Route 7. We must've seen the sign: "Oldest Covered Bridge in Massachusetts." We pulled over, parked the car and walked across it, then followed the dirt road that bisected cornfields before picking up the low meandering river alongside. I could not know then that in three years I would be living less than an hour from that bridge, that I would come to get my hair cut in the very same town. That six years from now, Mario would tell me that it had burned down. That he would whisper so low between hair snips I'd have to strain to hear: "The son of the man who owns the gas station across the street did it. He's gonna go on trial." A few haircuts later: "He was convicted, sentenced to jail." Later still: "He committed suicide. He hanged himself in jail." Mario couldn't tell me how he'd managed to do that. The whole town hated him it seemed. He was just sixteen.

The bridge is beautiful, with thick heavy beams that smell strongly of fresh wood, even now, eight years since it was reconstructed. A sign at the entrance tells of its past: "In 1994 it was burned down!" The perpetrator is not named. It seems wrong that his story is not told. I want there to be a marker for him as well, he whose name I do not know. A stone marker like the ones my friend and I saw in the ancient graveyards we walked through. The grass grows, perhaps even gets mowed, but the stone remains. Years later, centuries even, his name can be read. His story rubbed on a piece of paper with charcoal. Fire itself cannot erase it.

꙳

Meeting M.

At noon I checked out of the hotel. We were supposed to meet at Delaney's at one; I had already traced the route to get there. I knew her only from her book cover. I assumed I would recognize her—or she, me—we had exchanged books some months ago, then agreed to meet in this city—her city. Of course I would not stay with her—I was not on those kinds of terms; we had only written each other letters, e-mails. I had admired her books of stories, the elliptical way she had of writing. I'd come across an interview with her in a magazine somewhere, was attracted to her modesty, the painstaking care with which she wrote stories; I must have seen myself in her. "When you fall in love, you fall in love with yourself, when you kill yourself, you kill someone else." That silly refrain was stuck in my head now as I deposited my luggage in the trunk of my car, locked it and walked toward Delaney's. I was wearing new shoes, my feet felt tight and on the verge of blistering. I felt self-conscious about my weight; I was heavier than in my jacket photo.

I arrived at the restaurant before she did. At least I did not see her anywhere. I sat by the window so that I would see her approach—in a long skirt, I imagined, as in her photo, feet in something like Birkenstocks? I kept thinking she was late, but it was really me who had arrived too early and was now drinking cup after cup of coffee. I pictured myself in a sidewalk café in Paris rather than this sprawling city which I happened to be visiting (happened to be?) in Eastern Canada. It was not very attractive—the faint smell of sulfur, which reached me, it seemed, even inside the restaurant. She lived in an upscale neighborhood. Her husband (yes, she did have a husband) was, I think, a doctor.

I had told her I was en route to—what had I said?—a conference, which might have been true, except I doubted that I would ever arrive there. I would visit M. and then return home, or I would visit and then drive around aimlessly, pretending I had another destination. I would not let on that I no longer wrote, did not think myself a writer any longer.

"You're Clare, aren't you?"

I nodded, pulled out a chair for her. It bothered me that I hadn't seen her approach. She was not wearing the long skirt I had imagined, but sandals, yes (though not Birkenstocks), a summery blouse, pressed jeans.

"Did you sleep well? Was the hotel comfortable?"

We began with such pleasantries, inanities before ordering lunch from our hovering waiter.

She had this annoying habit of twisting a strand of her hair as she listened. It should have been charming, adolescent girllike, but it made me think she wasn't paying attention. I wanted to tell her to stop it. She neither looked nor acted as I'd imagined she would—a woman nearing 40—she seemed more like an uncertain girl.

Later I would realize that this was perhaps a defense mechanism on my part: a way not to fall in love with her. Concentrate on her flaws and I would not lose myself to her. But why drive more than 500 miles to reach that conclusion? I could not see it then.

Of course when I drove away I regretted that it hadn't gone better. The fact that she wanted to talk mostly about writing hadn't helped of course. I carried on some patter about the novel I was writing and watched her as I spoke, twisting a strand of hair round her finger—she seemed nervous, almost desperate.

Did she believe me? Could she tell I was fabricating everything, that writing was for me just the discussing of it? She had nice things to say about my previous books, carefully crafted phrases I did not take too seriously. She was flattered of course by my interest in her, in her work, in the stories that she wrote so beautifully.

"Will you try a novel?" I asked her.

"Oh! It takes me so very long just to write a story . . . Some have taken me years, you know I start them, go back to them, get stuck . . . I suppose I might, but I haven't really any "novel" ideas, I'm more of a poet, really, masquerading as a story writer . . ."

I thought she had a point there. "Shall we order dessert? Coffee?"

She ordered the crème brûlée; I followed suit. "What about you?" she asked. "Tell me about your own life . . ." as if we'd been talking about hers. We hadn't. I'd learned nothing of her husband, her daily life. I reminded myself to ask.

"Oh . . . quite dull really. . . . I'm divorced, have been for over five years. My life is really uneventful, the life of a small town . . ." The thought of my town made me feel ill suddenly. I'd lived there since my ex and I had left the city, then stayed on after the divorce when quite obviously, like a patch of poison ivy or a slice of moldy bread, it didn't agree with me. But then nothing seemed to agree with me. I was aware of that. I'd grown, more than ever, hard to please.

"It's a charming little village," I heard myself tell her. "You know, where everyone knows everyone else, the postmaster knows who's writing you letters and sending you packages, the neighbors check in on your cats while you're away . . ."

"Oh!" she said, "I might find that stultifying."

"Not at all! Reassuring really. To feel part of something—connected . . ."

"Well, yes, I suppose . . . though one has a bit of that here too, in the neighborhood . . ."

And so we continued in this mundane vein until "Is it influencing your fiction? Small town life?"

And I'd said yes, said some more about the novel I was writing (as I suddenly saw it): a thinly disguised village appearing at its center. I knew from previous publications how being a writer in a small town was both a curse and a blessing, and decided to shift the conversation to more solid footing. "Everyone wants to read what you're working on, then sees themselves in it even when they're not. The town wants to own you—this writer in their midst—as if you could bring some coinage to the town, put it on the map . . . but they rarely like what you've written. It's rather awkward. One misses the anonymity finally. . . ."

"Yes . . ." she said. "I can see that . . ." Then after a pause, "Do you ever get stuck? Lose the thread, find yourself unable to write?"

I shifted uncomfortably. How much should I tell her? "Well, yes, sometimes. . . . I find a long walk helps, or reading . . . What about you?"

She mumbled something I couldn't hear, spooned the last of her crème brûlée from the china dish. "It's always a struggle. One long struggle. Nothing enjoyable about it." She smiled then and I saw that she was really quite stunning.

I remembered to ask about her husband, the "quality of her days." I wanted her to be unhappy, but I cannot

honestly say that she was. She professed a good marriage, a love and respect for him. I felt myself wilting.
She had everything going for her, and it didn't look like
any of it was going to rub off on me, the smell of this
sulfur-city notwithstanding.

"Shall we walk for a bit? Before you head off? You're
heading to Halifax today is it?"

I nodded. We paid our bill, splitting it quite fairly
and without too much awkwardness.

It felt good to be out of the restaurant, the clinking
of china and silverware, the tinkling of conversation.

Strangely, we had trouble saying good-bye to one
another. We spoke of letters we would write, e-mails,
another visit possibly. "If you like, if you don't mind . . .
you could send me part of the novel you're working on?
I'd like to read it . . ."

I told her I'd consider it, that I didn't usually show
anything until I'd reached the end of it, and I was nowhere
near the end of my novel, was finding it very difficult,
troublesome, in ways the other novels hadn't been . . .

We said good-bye, a kiss on the cheek, a light hug
on the street corner. I watched her walk away. Was she
really 40? She looked no more than 26 to me.

It wasn't something I had planned, but as soon as
she'd left me, walked two blocks or so west, I began to
fall in step behind her. I thought I would see where she
was headed: was it home? Or did she have another appointment? I knew, like me, there were no children; at
least she had never mentioned any. I had nothing else

to do, and the thought of my car, the long drive home or some meandering drive to nowhere, disheartened me.

She did not seem in a hurry, stopping now and then to take in a store window: brightly colored leather purses and shoes; now a bookstore (would she venture in? No, she did not—). Not at all in a hurry to get back to home and husband—of course he must be at work. Her writing would be done for the day. She was a morning writer, an early riser. How clear her conscience must be—able to take in shoes and handbags! I envied that. I was in a muddle—that much was clear—or I would not be following her. And if she saw me? I had to take care that she did not. It would be the end of me. Exposed. The roots of a tree thrown up for all to see; the ugly veins beneath the opaque stockings

And now she was stopped before a chocolate shop. Was she really so self-indulgent? Or would she buy a gift for someone else—surely not her husband? I watched from a distance, took out my cell phone, dialed a random number as I slipped into a doorway, one that still offered me visibility.

She emerged, must have been ten minutes later—I didn't time it but so it felt—with a small package. What if it were meant for me? What if she sent it to me? This was crazy, she had no reason to indulge me . . . but I felt a flutter: a moth, not yet a butterfly of hope—and then I lost her. It could be argued that hope—however small—does that. It obscures reality. She had been in front of me, just two blocks away, and now I could not see her anywhere. Another store perhaps? A cross street? I pondered the possibilities and just as quickly lost interest. It wasn't right to be following. Quite wrong, intrusive really.

I went into the chocolate shop; I'd stock up for my long drive—I loved chocolate as much as the next person, more perhaps—especially the gourmet variety—wrapped as they were in blue and gold tinfoil. I felt strangely elated as I paid for my gift box, as if, in fact, she had already given it to me.

II
Meat Eaters & Plant Eaters

Meat Eaters & Plant Eaters

My cat is in the driveway, gnawing on fine bones. The rain has begun: a warm muzzled sound, large soft drips, not the rapid dark downpour of yesterday. Everything wet and green, sopping, soaking.

My cat comes in, sits on the desk where I write. His paw leaves a pale red print on the page. He wants to be scratched behind the ears, he splays himself belly up for extra attention. He thinks he lives a fine life and he does. Inside he is petted and catered to; outside he lives the secret life of a hunter.

Meat Eaters and Plant Eaters: my son has divided his dinosaurs into two collections, counts how many he has in each. Plant eaters are more pot-bellied we learn: huge stomachs to process all that scruffy plant material.

Meat Eaters are leaner, tougher, their bodies efficient hunting machines. My son likes the meat eaters best: their jagged teeth, fierce open jaws, arms outstretched for prey. He prefers predators to prey, words he's recently learned.

But in the morning: "Mom? What is that? What did I step on?"

And I clean his bare foot and the rug, now bloodstained, of the gizzards our cat left behind during the night. My son stares at what I flush away. "Was it a mouse?" "Yes, I think so."

It's summer and the dead things are multiplying: mice, a chipmunk, and if we are very unlucky: a small bird, its downy feathers floating in the house for days, like milkweed seeds come to rest

The cat has retired to the closet, kneads a sweater that's fallen over the tips of shoes. The pawing sets him purring, and soon he is curled into himself to sleep away the day.

"Are we going to die?" We are brushing our teeth, a ritual my son performs reluctantly, especially in the morning. "Are we going to die?" he asks again.

"Yes, but . . . not for a long long long time, not for maybe 100 years . . ."

"NO! We're not, we're *never* going to die."

Silence—we're both thinking—and then the question again: "Are we going to die?"

I hesitate—he's only five. "Yes, but . . ."

"NO!" and he pounds on my chest. What he doesn't

like he tries to pound right out of me. I know I need to talk to him about not hitting when he's mad, but for now I take the pounds. I go soft, evasive. "Maybe we won't die . . ." He must know I'm just saying that because he wants me to, I rationalize.

"*Never*. We're never going to die."

"Maybe . . ."

"Maybe means no. We're not going to die."

And that decides it. For now anyway. He's off to his bedroom, where his dinosaurs are. Craaak! I hear them crashing into one another, the Tyrannosaurus charging the Triceratops, but the Triceratops has horns and a thick skin, he may be able to get away alive. The swift meat eater catches him by the back leg, his teeth sink in; he bites a huge chunk of Triceratops; the poor plant eater will slowly die.

"I'm just going to drink water," my son tells me over lunch.

"And why is that?"

"Because if you drink water, you won't die."

I nod, wondering how he's reached this conclusion, then remember a book we read recently about the human body: we can live for so many days without food, but without water, we die. I pour another glass for him, glad that he prefers water to soda, at least for now.

From my window I catch sight of the cat outside. I watch him circle something in the tall grass. Quietly he paces, his circle tightening, closing in, and then quite suddenly he leaps, back arched. He's got something—though I can't see what—between his paws.

We find the something on the bathroom floor—this time abandoned, not eaten or opened, not even a bloody scar: a tiny brown field mouse, its tail a long wire. My son stares at it, watches as I gather it in a paper towel. "Is it alive? Are you going to let it go outside?" I nod, though I'm unsure whether it's dead or just stunned. I take the small bundle downstairs to thrust out the back door under the bushes outside.

"Did it get away?" my son asks.

I tell him that it did, though I didn't really see.

"Big plant-eating dinosaurs gulped down stones as they ate. The stones stayed in the gut, helping the stomach muscles grind leaves and twigs into a soft sticky stew of plants. Dinosaurs, such as Apatosaurus, could digest this stew more easily," I read from the thick book we got from the library, *All About Dinosaurs.*

"Apatosaurus used to be Brontosaurus. Read about the meat eaters now, Mom."

"Allosaurus had large eyes, nearly twice the size of those of the much bigger meat eater, Tyrannosaurus Rex. Above the eyes was a bony flap forming an eye ridge, possible to shade its eyes from the sun. Allosaurus had about 40 teeth in its upper jaw and 32 in its lower jaw. They were up to four inches long and their front and back edges were sharp and serrated, like steak knives, for slicing through flesh. As they wore out or broke, new teeth grew in their place . . ." I read on. The words do not seem to be putting my son to sleep; he's alert, intent on processing anything new we might learn. Our cat slips into the room through the closet door. He's found his way in, as he usually does, through the crawl space that leads through the attic, the attached garage, to the outside. He jumps onto the bed where we're sitting, slinks past us, his fur brushing against us in turn, as he makes his way to the end. He kneads himself a warm spot, and soon he is curled into himself, purring softly. My son likes that his bed has become the cat's favored resting spot.

"Shut the door Mom," he tells me as soon as I close the book.

I do, and from the other side I hear him slip out of the bed I've tucked him into, slam the closet door closed, then slip back in between covers. Now the cat is trapped in the room—no secret passageway to the nightworld outside. Most likely he hasn't realized this yet. I wonder how long he'll indulge my son, tolerate his constant stroking. For now they lie, two warm bodies fitted into one another: one purring, one stroking, soon twitching and dreaming.

⚯

The Voix Humaine

In those days, I walked alone. I did not want to be seen or spoken to. I lived with my cats, and we communicated contentedly among ourselves. I had decided they loved French best, and so I spoke in soliloquies to them, *"Ça va bien? Vous êtes bien, mes petits chats?"* and perhaps this made me feel less alone. But I did not really feel alone. I only wanted to hear sometimes the sound of the human voice, the *voix humaine.*

They did in fact know how to tell me what they knew. When they spied creatures lurking about on the property—a rabbit scurrying along the roadside, a deer who stood at attention in the dim light of a half moon— they growled, a low throaty sound, as they watched from their window perch. It was invariably loud enough to wake me if I was sleeping. They expected me to open the door and run the intruders off the property, as I had so often done with the shaggy black cat who'd been prowling and lurking ever since we'd taken up residence in our small home.

I fed them and they slept on either side of me, kept me company and, like me, they wanted no one else in our lives. When the plumber came, they hid under my bed until he had gone, while I did my best not to appear anxious, depressed, in front of this man who did not have the decency to wipe the mud off his shoes.

I no longer knew how to make small talk and wondered if I could get away without trying. There was of course the weather. I hadn't forgotten that chestnut: "Nice day, isn't it?" Or: "Terrible weather we're having . . ." but I felt weary of my voice before I even mouthed the words, and so eventually I too would go into the bedroom, lie on my bed, until my cats ventured out from under, dust on their foreheads, to keep me company.

Make a Nest

It's easy to look back and not understand. As a child I used to steal robin's eggs and smash them. I wasn't allowed to touch the nest—there were bugs inside, my mother warned. "What kind of bugs? Where?" Nothing you could see—invisible gnats, spiders, things that would sicken you . . . I envisioned gnats crawling all over me, settling down somewhere—my hair perhaps, my armpits, behind my knees—they'd discover a home, they'd make their nest right on me.

If we'd had a cat, the cat would've killed the birds and that would be that. But cats were not allowed. Hated creatures by my father who preferred dogs. A dog would follow you around all day, tripping over your heels so you could get annoyed that the dog had no life of its own but secretly glad, very glad, it followed you everywhere.

My son's new friend is the daughter of one-time circus performers. We bring her back to her house, climb the basement stairs, notice the windowsill lined with nests, small and tinier: homes woven from twigs, grasses and stray feathers, thread, bits of plastic. There are eggshells nestled there—pale blue and broken of course; the birds themselves hatched, stolen or fallen—in any case, long gone. We stand on the stair, transfixed by this display, at once delicate and haphazard, lovely and dusty.

I own cats—two—and so the birds cannot frequent the feeder we hang from the eaves over our front door. Even so, the birdseed has gone down. Silently, unseen, birds must be feeding themselves. I sit on a lawn chair in the yard, cat curled in my lap, listen to the traffic streaming by, and wonder how so many birds can thrive so close to town. I hear them, though I cannot see them, in the canopy of leaves: calling or singing. I don't know enough to name them from their sounds.

A scene in a film I recently saw: an Iranian boy, blind, waits by himself in a city park for his father to fetch him from school. He hears something, is driven into the bit of woods, stops to shoo away the cat, arms before him, feeling as he goes. He finds the tree, gropes the leaves beneath it. At last his fingers touch the bird, fallen from its nest (but how could he know that sound?), scrawny and helpless. He places it carefully in his shirt pocket, climbs the tree to return it to its nest.

My son won't watch the film with me, or only half an hour of it. It is full of sadness; the father clearly wants his blind son to be gone, thinks his life will fall into place without him. When the film ends, my son wants me to watch *Bubble Boy* with him; I refuse, though later I realize I ought to have let myself enter that world—silly and brash though I find it—as he did mine, if only for half an hour.

My son's new friend would have loved *Bubble Boy*. She is being brought up without Hollywood, without candy or television. Next year she will be home-schooled. At home only French is spoken. She is Fauve, named after the *Fauvistes*, the "wild beasts" of expressionism.

There is a painting I wanted to own, the only one I've ever bid on (a silent auction), a very small painting, no larger than a book or a stone: a bird nest painted in thick white paint, a background of blue. I hadn't realized I wanted to own such a thing. But how could I know until I saw it painted? I didn't win of course. There were those willing to pay more than I, others who wanted a nest of their own.

I have my own nest now. It rests next to the cracked teapot in the corner of a far shelf. From where I sit I can see it, nestled in its new home. It was winter when I found it. Even until recently (late March) the ice and snow have held everything in their grip—as if we lived in Minnesota, Montana or Buffalo, instead of the northwest corner of Connecticut. I saw it—a dark mass against the white, tucked into the branches of a small tree. I reached up for it and the vines that had wrapped themselves around the trunk did not want me to have it. Prickers ripped my sleeve, pulling at the jacket I wore, and when I removed my gloves to better grasp it, thorns snagged me.

It wasn't mine, I knew. But then it was no one else's either: expertly woven from reed grass, twigs and leaves, filled with freshly fallen snow. When the snow melted: a nest of berries, nuts and seeds.

Make a nest.

A friend, divorced, no girlfriend, writes me late at night, thoughts rambling: "In nature, creatures with eyes on opposite sides of the head, like birds, or fish (not flounders), are that way because they are prey. The prowlers have eyes in front. It seems women should have eyes on opposite sides of their heads (I know I sound insane now). What's the deal with "the chase"? I watch *Forbidden Planet* and all the men are practically sexually harassing Anne Francis and stalking her. Uma Thurman in an interview a while ago, long ago, talked of how (and my ex talked of this too), you've got to "make a nest" for women to be interested: "They say that if it's happy hour at the Disco/Bar, the women there, if they see a guy with a paunch, think, 'He's too slow to hunt for food.' But I've also thought this: They might reconsider. Say an affluent man/hunter has a big belly because he's got all this food . . . so they say, 'He's got food, he can feather the nest.'"

I have a different association with nests, one I realized some years ago, then wondered why I had not realized it before; it seemed quite obvious. I was unhappily married, the marriage already on its last legs, its knees, or down at the ankles—the metaphor is yours to choose. I dreamed of the man I was in love with, the one I corresponded regularly with, and satisfying my needs as I lay in bed (daytime, alone), the image of a bird nest came to me: a bird in its nest, an egg too. The image came, and stayed.

A private association, one I never told anyone. How astonished I was when last spring I heard my friend Sean Dougherty read his poem, "Erotic Poem," publicly,

> *My hand is a starfish between your legs.*
> *A bird's nest made of rain.*
> *In the far-off trees, the tiniest egg falls.*
> *When you come I hear it cracking.*

In class the next day, one of my students (an older woman) said, "I've never heard such erotic poetry—how does he know my secret fantasies?" Of course I did not own the image—it was hers—and if hers, just as surely, others'.

My Mom from Budapest

When I was small, not yet school age, my mother used to regularly take me to cafés, sometimes traveling as far as an hour to reach one we'd never been to. She seemed to be preparing me for a life of cafés, or perhaps she was only nostalgic for the days when she herself would frequent them in cities where she'd once lived. We would spend hours there—oddly, I don't recall being bored. She would order her café latte or cappuccino, and I'd have my hot cocoa or warm milk with honey, and then we'd sit at the small table (she let me choose) by the window or in the far corner. Sometimes there were magazines to thumb through, sometimes even a shelf of books, including children's, but she would never read to me in this setting—I knew that somehow—perhaps

I'd asked her to repeatedly until I learned. She really wouldn't do anything other than dreamily sip her coffee, stare out the window, watch the other customers. Once it may have bothered me—her obliviousness of me, her almost complete lack of engagement—but I grew used to it, for I don't remember demanding her anything. I think I must have fallen into my own reverie, and that became what we shared: a dreamy state we'd sink down into, then reluctantly slip out of. I think now she must have been imagining herself in Paris, in Barcelona or Madrid—the truth is we were living in a small town surrounded by farm plots. Not far away were the tractors plowing the fields, overturning manure-laden earth; the smell was pungent. As a small boy I thought the world of those machines, knew all the makes by heart: Allis-Chalmers, International, Kubota, Massey Ferguson, and, of course, the green giant: John Deere. My mother did not discourage this interest, though it must have hurt her heart to see me so enthralled by something like farm machinery.

Once in a very great while my father came with us, but he lacked the knack for just sitting, and soon after the coffee was drunk—and mother always had to drink it faster than she would normally—he would stand up, reach for his wallet: it was time to head for the door. Those visits always felt aborted to me—painfully short, and I'm sure my mother felt so too; it became a ritual we indulged in only privately.

As I grew older I used to wonder what she'd done before I was born: what had she been doing in all those faraway cafés—besides drinking coffee? But she would tell me she did nothing more than what we did together: sit, drink in the atmosphere. I sometimes wondered, if a war were going on around us, if a bomb were suddenly dropped outside our café, would my mother continue sitting? I think I believed she would have. Of course no bombs ever fell, but sometimes a storm would gather out of nowhere and great raindrops would fall and splatter, as thunder broke loudly, terrifically, outside our café. My mother would smile at me then: "Isn't it delicious? To be here inside on such a day?" Of course at home we had left the windows wide open in the sweltering heat, but she was not one to think about that, to race home to close windows, to save floorboards and carpet from a downpour—and as a child, of course neither was I. The rain was pelting outside the window by which we sat, sluicing down the glass, and we were watching as we held our warm mugs between our hands; it seemed nothing could be more wonderful than that.

Sometimes a waiter would approach our table, "Can I get anything else for you and your boy?" And my mother would smile at him, shake her head no. Perhaps because her reverie had been interrupted, she'd soon launch into stories, "You know in Budapest the waiters wear little vests and hats . . . In Cracow they drink coffee out of cups the size of thimbles and the coffee is so strong—so strong—they put a rind of lemon in it . . . In Paris there are little triangle plots for gardens—you can see them from the trains—people grow lettuce, cucumbers, beets in a triangle no bigger than this table . . ." Later I would find out she had been to hardly any of these places, but at the time I believed her. She was the authority, after all, on the Great Beyond—my father never spoke of such things. He had traveled some, but that was a long time ago—his world was very much the present one: the small town that we lived in, his work as a contractor. For my mother, however, these places were ever present in her mind, more vivid perhaps than the town we lived in. She would let her mind wander, far from the farm fields and small town where we lived, down dim alleys and lanes, crowded marketplaces, odd shops and buildings, and I liked it when she took me along. Even now I can picture the places she'd describe: a sod house on a dirt road where a leathery old man made shoes with wooden soles, though no one bought them anymore—he'd been making them since the war; a closet-sized store stocked with hundreds of button-filled glass jars, a multitude of colors, shapes and sizes, so many that they spilled onto the floor; a market where pigs' heads and skinned rabbits—still with the fur on the paws—lay waiting for you to pull out your wallet and buy them . . .

Sometimes my mother would tell me something of the years she spent as a young girl with her family abroad—she had told me that for a short time they lived in Amsterdam—describing for me the house of yellow brick, the fantastic head of a lion carved above the door, the canal with its barges and houseboats, a sound of water lapping as if just outside their door. Years later I would discover that only one summer of her childhood was spent abroad; she'd grown up in Cleveland, Ohio. I know now what (who) the fantasy was attached to, but I could not then, and even if she had hinted, whispered in my ear, "I'm making this part up, it's not really my life, but someone else's . . . ," I wouldn't have found that strange, as the line between stories real and imagined was for me not a significant one. Children who deny having crayoned the wall, who insist someone else did it—Tommy Crayon, for instance, which is what I said (I am told—I do not remember)—do not consider themselves liars. They fabricate to protect themselves with the instinct that any other act of self-defense requires. In this way, I imagine my mother and I were perfect companions for one another. She understood my "lies," and I never questioned—how could I have known enough to?—her own exaggerations.

Mom had her favorite cafés, the old standbys, but more often than not we'd venture off in search of a new one, a café-restaurant she'd heard about, or seen an ad for somewhere. We'd navigate back roads to get to a town we'd never been to previously, locate the establishment, the requisite cappuccino, and then find ourselves the only customers.

"What a quiet day for Fayetteville!" the waitress-owner would say, as if every day were not like this; even then I think I knew that the new establishments never lasted. But my mother would act as if it were otherwise; as if she were watching a couple or an elderly gentleman at the next table, as if, surrounded by the buzz and hum of chatter in a smoke-filled café, she were listening in on someone's conversation. In reality the place was deserted, as was the town. I sipped my cocoa, let my mother "soak in the atmosphere," though of course there was very little, none to speak of. At the local hardware store there was a lot more action; the overflowing parking lot was proof of this, if proof were needed. People were stocking up on supplies: things for building, remodeling, repairing, which is what one did in our town. Our own home was neglected; it lacked a garden and the perpetual lawn care nearly everyone else indulged in. Doing such things would of course leave Mom little time for her cafés.

Now I look back and think why didn't she get involved? I don't mean the gardens, horses, houses and barbecues everyone else was busy with, but there must have been something—the library, a bookstore, a course somewhere she could take or even teach; she was good at languages. But she didn't try any of these. She must have liked living on the outskirts. She was like a Russian immigrant landed from a faraway city, she did not speak the language or know the customs; fear or her age or stubbornness?—made her cling to her foreignness.

Few friends ever came home with me when I was a child; with a mother who did not mingle, who acted like she'd just arrived from Budapest, my friends' parents must have seen her as she appeared: aloof, unapproachable, impenetrable. I remember some crazy arguments between her and Dad: Why couldn't she talk to the woman who cut my hair, who was so friendly? Why couldn't she meet with my kindergarten teacher? Become friends with other mothers?

In Dad's mind it was all a ruse—an excuse not to get involved in the community, or even in their marriage—I know that now. In his mind, she was holding herself back, unwilling to commit herself, to take on this landscape as her own. Which could only have been extremely frustrating for him. All of which, it seems to me, explains the dog. The dog was his attempt to root her, just as perhaps I had been but could not—alone—do (Had he also wanted other children? Given in to her refusal?). Of course a dog was really such an odd choice, and only made her further removed. But once it arrived, there was no going back to undo it.

And so one day out of nowhere, with no previous discussion or announcement (at least none that involved me), Dad came home with a puppy. I was ecstatic: I'd always wanted one and never dreamed I'd get it—I'm not even sure I had the courage to make my wishes known. So it was as if Christmas had suddenly arrived out of season.

As a child I loved that dog. Not having any siblings, and only very rarely a playmate, I needed Mocha. That was his name: Mocha. It was true he was brownish-black, but Mom's name for him seemed to be an attempt to draw him into our café-circle, to mark him as part of our almost daily ritual. But of course he could not enter. Once, and only once, we took him with us. I'm sure I insisted, but I know Mom also wanted to believe it would work—that our almost daily adventures could go on uninterrupted. In the car he jumped all over me, and once he hurtled himself into the front seat, nearly causing Mom to go off the road. At the café, we carefully tied him to a post outside, entered the establishment and ordered our hot drinks, only to find ourselves prisoners of his constant barking, his endless struggles with the leash—he looked as if he would soon strangle himself—and finally I had to abandon my hot chocolate in order to rescue him from his suicidal lashings.

And that was what began to happen: more and more often I traded Mom and our café outings for Mocha. It was as if the dog had broken the bubble of our days; he just crashed into the sleepy-dreaminess of it all, and the bubble was far too delicate, too ethereal, to ever be reconstructed. Mocha was something wild and alive, constantly jumping all over me. He needed my attention, and I loved that he did. "Sit! Down! Paw! Give me your paw!" I'd command loudly, briskly, before rewarding him with food, just as Dad had taught me, and Mocha watched and listened and obeyed me. His behavior thrilled me.

For a time Mom did make an effort with him—I'll be the first to say that she did. She and I would take Mocha for walks down the country roads around where we lived—she was finally doing what everyone else did—but somehow the dog knew not to obey her. Cars seldom passed by and when one did, Mocha was off and running behind it, leash trailing after him. "Mocha!" she'd yell, "Bad dog!" for he had ripped from her. But he didn't listen and rarely came when she called him. Once he ran in front of a car, and the driver had to slam on his brakes, making tracks on the road. "Can't you curb your dog? Don't you know how to walk one?" he yelled. I'd never heard anyone yell at her, not even Dad. Even when they argued, he never yelled at her. Sometimes he raised his voice, but more often exasperation outweighed anger, and he was never nasty.

All the way home Mom said nothing to me—too bruised, hurt, or angry—angry at Dad most of all perhaps, for getting the dog in the first place. And after that, there was no more dog walking.

Of course that had been the whole point to begin with: to get Mom outside and involved, but Dad should have realized a dog was not the sort of thing to accomplish this. Even I could see that there was nowhere for a dog to fit in the picture she had constructed of herself, and I do blame Dad for not realizing that. But then, he had his own picture, and as he saw it, it was theirs, a picture they'd constructed together: Why couldn't she at least make an attempt to remain part of it?

It must have been around this time that the nature of my excursions changed; it was no longer a café, that indoor almost urban world, but the woods across the road on which my journeys centered. I would take Mocha by the leash and the two of us would wander the trails that crisscrossed through the forest. I'd notice turkeys: huge and clumsy, they'd try to lift their bodies to take flight when they heard us. I found frogs, giant mushrooms, and underground holes. I imagined families of woodchucks, moles, foxes—even snakes, all living in a labyrinthine network of underground tunnels and passageways. It was an underground metropolis, one I was sure Mocha and I were walking on the ceiling of as we tromped through the woods. Perhaps they were my mother's images after all, but driven underground: the narrow streets and towering buildings she'd described were for me the dens and palaces of animals down below.

She did not accompany me. More than ever I wish she had. I feel certain she would have learned to like it, to love it even, as I did: the feel of crisp leaves underfoot, the crackle of branches and call of unseen birds, the very aliveness of the forest. But she refused. And so it was Mocha who joined me, and when he got home from work, my Dad. Dad was himself most of all in the forest. Just as Mom needed that hint of smoke, of caffeine, to feel that she was really breathing, Dad needed the outdoors. The air was crisp and clean, cold in our nostrils, and the two of us would pretend to be hunting a great bear; Mocha was our lookout. He'd run ahead (in the forest we let him off his leash), and we pretended he was on the Great Bear's scent; at any moment he would come running back to tell us where it was hiding.

For a while, probably longer than anyone else would have, Dad tried to include her. "We're going to walk Mocha. Aren't you coming?" Dad would say to her, waiting as we stood at the door, our hats and gloves already on; it was December. "Aren't you coming this time?" he'd say again, ignoring the look on her face, which clearly told him she had no intention, had never had one.

"No, not now," she'd say, stifling a yawn. "I should probably get our dinner ready."

Both of us knew perfectly well she wasn't going to spend her time cooking while we were away. She disliked cooking, and though she did do it for our sakes, it was almost always the simplest dishes you could imagine. What did she do those long hours when we were gone? I suppose she read. She had a number of books in French and Spanish; she liked to sit with these, to savor them slowly, though I'm not at all sure she ever read her way through one. But perhaps she deserves more credit than I give her.

Once she did come with us. She would let herself try things once—only once—a one-time trial that she'd agree to, and always it failed, failed very grandly. It must have been during hunting season, or worse perhaps: the season hadn't yet started. The three of us made our way down the dirt road that petered into various trails through the woods. I stepped on puddles frozen in old tire tracks, listened to the satisfying crack of ice-glass. Mocha ran ahead, coming back to us every so often, most of all to sniff Mom; he seemed more astounded than anyone that she'd agreed to join us. I was trying to point out to her the allure of the forest: the various kinds of bushes and trees (ignorant though I was of their names), the place where I'd seen a turkey break into clumsy flight, then drop one of its feathers down to me as a souvenir (I was sure).

We noticed Mocha had stopped doubling back. We couldn't see him, so we called for him to rejoin us, our voices echoing through the forest. Still he didn't appear, and we walked on, our eyes and ears open and searching. Not much farther ahead it became clear what had detained him: a doe had been shot. She lay to one side of the road with ankles tied together, as if someone had been called away in the middle of dragging her off. Crows or vultures had already picked at her entrails, which trailed from a bloody hole, and her eyes were open wide, stunned and silent. I touched her fur before Mom pulled me away, and it wasn't soft as I'd imagined, more like a bristly brush. Her mouth was open, the spit dried down one side, and I remembered the story Dad had told me about how he'd accidentally hit a deer with his van, and at the moment of impact, the deer's saliva had arced then fallen back, a fine sticky spray that had covered his windshield. That story had been fantastic to me; I'd imagined the deer again and again at the moment of impact: its body arching into the air, then falling back in a tremendous crash (in my mind it was not the spit but her body which had arced and fallen back). Dad had shown me where it occurred and whenever we drove by the spot, I'd see the accident as I'd imagined it happening: in terrible yet fantastic slow motion.

But I'd never actually seen it, not the accident nor even its aftermath. And now here lay a deer, somehow both more beautiful and ugly than I'd pictured. For a moment we said nothing, stunned into silence. Except for Mocha. He'd already pulled some entrails out through the hole in the deer's sides, his nose a bloody rose, and he tugged them loose before scampering into the woods with his prize.

It was Dad's and my job to get Mocha back to the house and away from the deer. Mom had long ago left us alone with the task. "This is awful, revolting . . . ," she'd said, and we couldn't tell if she meant Mocha, or the deer, or all of it. "I can't stand it—I'm going back." Dad said nothing, engrossed as he was in trying to get Mocha away from the woods and the bloody deer parts.

She didn't join us again on our daily walks. "I'm not interested in dead animal parts," was the line she gave us, and of course after a while we got tired of that line, and Dad no longer even asked her.

What remains mysterious to me is whether she kept up her café ventures without me. I suppose she must have: What else was there to keep her occupied? A look at the speedometer of her car would have of course answered this question. But as a child I would never have thought to do that; I may not even have had the curiosity. It was left to my father to do that sort of investigating. I myself had started school and so was gone for the good part of the day, and while Mom was always happy to see me when I returned, even tried to lift me up in her arms (I was a heavy boy by then and getting taller), it was never quite the same between us, the way it had been before, when the smell of coffee, the sound of other voices, the indoor atmosphere, was enough to make us forever and supremely happy, with no other need but our own company.

Fruits of the Dead

"Once before you were born, when I was five or six months pregnant, I spent an afternoon in a cemetery." Her son, just turned four, liked nothing better than to hear a story that involved himself, his younger self. "Tell me about when I had a fever," he'd said just the other day, "how my teacher called you and you got a phone call in your class . . ." She'd told him that story many times—it all became story—how she had to leave her students in the middle of a lecture to pick him up and take him to the doctor. He'd been miserable, had thrown a tantrum in the car; she'd barely been able to get him out of the car and into the doctor's (and then everyone staring at them in the waiting room, as if no one else had a child who'd ever misbehaved publicly).

"This was a cemetery in London, a city faraway . . ."
She suddenly couldn't remember what had brought her
there—and without her husband? She remembered she'd
been walking and walking; she'd worn the wrong shoes,
sandals that her heels kept slipping out of. At last she'd
found the graveyard—had she been looking for it all
along? Had that been her destination, the purpose behind
all that walking? She couldn't remember. What she did
remember were the berries: big thick juicy blackberries,
plumper and tastier than any she'd ever eaten. Purple
juice stained her hands, and still she couldn't stop picking them, devouring them by the handful. She'd felt so
hungry, she couldn't get enough of them, though all the
while she was thinking, these are only so plump and
tasty because they're growing out of the rotting dead.
It seemed wrong, not healthy, to be feeding her unborn
child—so greedily—the fruits of dead people. Though
she did not stop herself.

Her legs had hurt, her feet and legs swollen, and
the urge to lie down on top of one of the tombstones,
granite warmed by the sun, and close her eyes, almost
overwhelmed her. The other visitors—stray couples and
families—kept her from giving in. She noticed that one
family, Iranian maybe (why did she think that?), had
brought buckets with them. They were blackberry picking in the cemetery. . . . And she'd been furtive, stealing
berries by the handful, eating them as she walked where
no one would see her, holding back, pretending to study
a gravestone, when really it was the blackberry bush

bending over it that interested her. Yet this family made no attempt to hide the purpose of their outing. Still, she felt odd, not right, though she did not stop herself.

"And now do I like berries?"

"You like them a lot. Remember in the summertime we go across the road to find them in the woods?"

"Yes, and we bring a cup to put them in."

But they were straggly and few. Often sour, picked before they were ready, and never profuse. Not lush like those in London, but she and her son picked them anyway, because scavenging for food gave them something to do.

"Mom, you know what?"

"What?" she asked her son, her mind distracted, lingering still among the gravestones.

"You forgot something."

"What? What did I forget?" she asked, looking at him now, her eyes searching his as they sat next to one another on the living room couch.

"You forgot to tell me about the cats."

"Oh . . . ," she said, "you're right—I did."

And so she had. One story always followed the other; that is how she had told it the first time, so that was how she must tell it again.

"Well," she said, "let me see. . . . The cats came much later, you know, it was just last year . . . suddenly we had so many, a whole family. . . ."

First, a pregnant cat had found them—no, she wasn't pregnant, she'd just given birth, and was on the search for food. She'd been left behind; they'd found her nest with five kittens in the ransacked trailer down the road. They'd taken all six cats in, hoping to find homes for them.

"And what about Bones? You forgot Bones, Mom . . ."

"Oh yes, Bones . . . ," she said, more to herself than him. "Well, one day, not long after we found the kittens, a hungry black cat just showed up, out of nowhere . . ." A cat they'd never once seen before, just black fur stretched over bones, so skinny you could see his every rib. They fed him and he longed to be taken into their home, petted and cuddled, but with three cats of their own, the mama cat and her kittens, she could find no room for him. She was constantly thrusting him out (he slunk in as she held the door open for her son), but he was so persistent, tenacious: crying at the door, then hanging by his claws on the screen window as they ate their breakfast—as if in someone's nightmare—that it seemed cruel not to give in. But she was resolved; he would live in the garage until they found a home for him. He soon grew to a normal size, his black fur thick and shiny again, but she could never get rid of that other image of him, wasted and starving, crying at the door and hanging at the window.

They had tried to get rid of them, and had found homes for two kittens, but the others . . . no one wanted them, no one at all; not even the animal shelter would take them. The shelter had so many different stories: "There's an infectious disease going around right now . . ."

"There's been a fire in the basement . . ." "Our cats are in quarantine . . ." "We have a moratorium on cats right now . . ." *Quarantine, moratorium,* she was sure they just threw around these terms to scare away callers.

Once she saw a notice in the papers about a black cat that had disappeared; the couple was "desperately searching." Suddenly hopeful, she'd called them. On the phone she saw that Bones didn't quite fit the description (no patch of white fur under his chin), but she sensed the couple's eagerness to believe otherwise, and invited them over to see him. For once Bones sat in their living room, licking and preening himself in a cushioned chair, looking as if he'd always belonged there.

Despite his inattention to them, his smaller size and lack of a white patch, the couple almost convinced themselves that Bones was their Blackie. She found herself encouraging them, and when this didn't work (they suddenly emerged, as if from a dream, to announce, "No, it isn't him"), "Well, why don't you take him anyway? He's friendly and neutered. I'm afraid you won't find your Blackie . . ." But they left empty-handed.

And then the mama cat got pregnant again. Looking at the cat's swollen belly made her feel ill. Why on earth hadn't they thought to neuter her? Any day there would be even more cats to contend with. "You have to do something," she told her husband. "I don't care what it is . . ."

He made an appointment with the veterinarian. He never described the procedure, only that he'd walked into an office with an armful of live cats, then walked out with two cardboard carrying cases, very heavy ones. There were people in the waiting room—he'd wondered what they were thinking.

"And then Dad buried them . . ."

"Yes, he took them to the woods." He hadn't described that part to her either, hadn't wanted to. It was something he'd done for her. He'd carried the cardboard cases and a shovel across the road. In a secluded spot in the woods, one not visible from the road, he'd dug a wide hole, then emptied the contents of the two cases in. The bodies fell one on top of the other; the last was Bones, now a good solid weight, his shiny black fur covering up the smaller bodies. Digging farther in the woods, he'd found more dirt and leaves to bury them with. Deep enough, he thought. But walking the path in the woods some weeks later, he'd noticed vultures. What could those birds be after? Without thinking, they'd gone over to investigate. She hadn't wanted her son to see, to know, but it was too late: the giant birds were chewing on small bones.

"What are all those bones? Where did all those bones come from?" their son had asked, and she and her husband had exchanged glances. "You deal with this one," her husband's look said, "this is your doing." And so she told her son the story because that is what she'd always done.

"Mom," her son said, nudging her again, "Let's go look for berries now."

"Yes, we'll go," she answered, though it wasn't time—too soon, the sun too faint. The fruits would be only green and bitter versions of themselves, she knew.

III
Close Your Eyes

Hans & His Daughter

I

One day his wife didn't come back.

Hans paced the room uneasily, calculating time in his head: two flights of stairs, five blocks to the grocery, a few things to choose from, maybe some remarks to that man at the store? The baby's crying interrupted his thoughts.

"You shouldn't cry," he said, "you're two years old now." He picked her up, then put her down. She cried even harder. "Sophie, Sophie, Sophie, Sophie," he said. He carried her around the room as he paced, walking in step to her crying.

He recalculated, adding the five blocks back, then stopped. From his window he watched the man selling flowers at the end of the block. Could she have stopped to buy flowers? He imagined her choosing a rose, pulling it gently from a cluster of others, then let the image slip from his mind. Buying flowers couldn't account for all that time. But maybe someone had grabbed her, led her somewhere—down an alley, or to a strange part of town. It must be some man who had tricked her, someone with nothing but lies.

Hans shuddered and closed his eyes. Could this have happened? He had to find out. He had to find his wife.

He started for the door. Ah, no, he thought, I must write a note, so she doesn't think, "My husband's run off with my child." He scribbled it out: "Where are you? We've gone to find you," and signed his name.

"Sophie, you want to sign this note to Mommy? Yes?" He placed the pencil in her fist and held it so she could write. Sophie slid her fist across the page, and when Hans lifted the paper, her mark went on the table.

"Oh Sophie, Sophie, Sophie, silly girl," he said, and gathered her in his arms. She struggled all the way downstairs, but he held onto her.

"Now look for Mommy," he told her as he let her down outside. Sophie began to cry, "Mommy, I want Mommy." She wouldn't move, though he tried to lift her. She had planted herself firmly on the sidewalk, her weight keeping her glued there. "I want Mommy."

Hans pleaded and pulled at her, but Sophie refused to move. He looked around for help, and seeing no one, he left her—just for a moment. He ran to the end of the street, glanced to the right and the left. He scanned the streets for his wife, the woman with the plain blue dress, the straight brown hair. He looked up and down fire escapes, into doorways and parked cars. Hans saw that this part of town held no trace of her, and he began to worry about his daughter.

A woman, older than he with short grey hair, stood before his daughter. Hans could hear her voice, slow and even, as he neared. "Mommy will come any minute now, I know she will. She's looking in all the stores for you. She's just around the corner, I know she is."

Sophie nodded her round face, holding tightly to some tissues in one hand, some candies in yellow cellophane in the other. Hans stood listening. Perhaps his wife was just around the corner, perhaps this woman knew . . .

The woman met his eyes. "We should call the police," she said in a quiet tone, "the girl's been abandoned."

"Oh no," Hans blurted, almost stammering. "No please, I'm her father."

The woman looked from Hans to his daughter, "I see," she said, staring once more, then left them alone.

Sophie had begun to cry again, "Mommy, I want Mommy," and Hans said, "Ssshh, we'll find her," and tried to lift her, but she was still planted firmly. He struggled with his child, tugging at her hands, her arms. Crouching, he looked into her eyes.

"Come, Sophie, we'll find Mommy, she's home now, let's go home." He opened one of the cellophane wrappers to give her a candy, and pushed it past her teeth to stop her crying. Sophie looked at him through blurred eyes as she clutched and unclutched the tissues and let herself be carried.

He walked back to the house thinking yes, of course, his wife was home now. But when he tried the door, it was locked, and when he turned the key, no one greeted him from inside. It was just as they had left it, with the note and Sophie's mark on the table.

He was hungry. He looked through the refrigerator—a bit of milk, some eggs. He didn't know how to cook much, but he could, he thought, cook an omelet for the two of them.

When they had finished eating, Hans wondered what to do. Did his wife put her to bed? It seemed likely, though he couldn't remember exactly. But Sophie screamed when he tried to lay her down. Well, if one isn't tired, one can't sleep, he thought, bringing her back to the living room. How could she not be tired? He was tired, as he sat in the chair by the window. He felt he would sleep as soon as he closed his eyes. But he watched the window, watched the people walking by—was one among them his wife? He listened to their steps fall away. No one, not one, turned to come in, to climb the steps to his room. He watched the night darken as Sophie sat in his lap, closing her eyes without meaning to, breathing aloud, a sleepy nasal breath.

When he realized she was sleeping, that the dark had settled outside and in the room, Hans grew scared.

Tomorrow was Monday. He would have to work tomorrow. He placed Sophie in bed and lay on his own. He tried to imagine his wife in another part of town. He saw her holding roses, standing among bushels of flowers. He watched her face, pale with blue eyes, surrounded by thick scents and colors. Her face faded then, and Hans tried to retrieve her from all those flowers, but the roses overpowered her.

II

Hans woke to the sound of his daughter's crying. He noticed this first and then, that the bed was empty beside him. It was early morning. He should be dressed, ready for work. And Sophie? He could call in sick.

He dressed and hurried downstairs to a phone booth. He dialed the print shop. "I'm sick from a diseased goat," he said. "Yes, I ate goat's cheese that was from a sick goat . . . yes, yes, but it's not too serious. I'll recover in another day . . . yes, I'm sure, quite sure." He hung up the phone and rushed upstairs.

It bothered him that he'd lied. But it *had* happened once, only that was when he was a small boy in the country. He felt so tired; perhaps I am sick, he thought, and it seemed he might be, the way the walls closed in around him.

Food, he thought, yes, that would help. But there was none in the house. They had so little money, and he was losing it now, with every minute that ticked away; there would be no hours to punch in on his time card. He pulled Sophie out of bed. Her face was red from crying, and her eyes looked sore. It had worn her out—all that crying. She let herself be dressed, carried downstairs and outside.

Hans remembered the man with the flowers. His heart beat faster as he wondered how to approach him. But in the next block, Hans saw that the man wasn't there. He tried to remember if there was a day of the week the man didn't come—was it a Monday?—and held tightly to his daughter's hand as they walked by.

At the grocery, Hans paced up and down the aisles, unsure what to buy. At last he chose some bread, some leafy vegetables, a few cans and jars. He paid for these and then asked quickly, "Did you see my wife yesterday, a woman with long brown hair?" The grocer only stared, said, "No . . . ," and Hans walked abruptly toward the door.

He made eggs and toast, coffee for himself, hot milk for his daughter. She was hungry now, not like before when she let him finish her plate; she ate almost greedily. He felt some pride as he watched her eat, and some other foreign feeling, as if he were watching someone who wasn't his daughter, not two years old at all. When she looked up at him with her large brown eyes, Hans looked quickly to the window. He felt a sudden anger welling up—that she should keep him in this small house, when he needed to be out, at work, away from her. It made him tired—this cooking and staying inside. He would do it differently tomorrow. He would have to think of something. And she kept looking up at him with large expectant eyes.

"What do you want, Sophie," he said, and as she looked up at him, her lip began to sink lower, and then she closed her eyes. Hans listened to her cry, wondering what to do.

III

He took her to the park, pushed her on the swing. Sophie laughed each time the swing lifted her into the air. He pushed her for a long time, glad to hear her laughter as she sailed forward and backward.

He brought her to the sandbox to play while he sat on a bench with a group of mothers. He watched her imitate the two boys, packing the dirt with her chubby hands, as he listened to the mothers describe their sons and daughters.

Sophie was digging up handfuls of dirt and throwing them all around her. She laughed to see it fall through the air. A small boy was struck by a handful, and he wiped his face and started to cry.

"It's in my eye!" he cried, and the mothers jumped forward to rescue the boy while Hans tried to lift his daughter. Sophie kicked and shouted, "No, no!" Hans felt the mothers' eyes on him as he struggled with his child, but they said nothing, only turned to look as he walked away.

At home he tried to entertain her, but he was tired and could think of no stories to tell or amusing things to show her. He thought, as he made dinner for the two of them, he would have to learn to cook more. As for him—he didn't care—could live on eggs and meat and meat and eggs, but maybe it wasn't good for a child? These things he didn't know.

The day had been long, much longer than any day he knew at work. At least there he was busy, and he didn't mind being always occupied. But today had been filled with endless worrying. Tomorrow will be different, he thought, as he lay down to sleep.

IV

He brought her to work.

"Back to work?" they said, "Feeling better?" Then noticed the child tugging at his arm.

"Well, yes, I'm fine now, but my wife, she's very sick. I couldn't leave my daughter with her. I had to bring her along . . ." He felt his face redden. He hated to lie. They shrugged their shoulders.

He left Sophie in the lobby with some magazines. But it was no use—he could hear her crying above the sound of the printer's machinery. It tangled in the machines, and he couldn't run them, listening to her. He slowed down until he had to stop and see if she wouldn't quiet down, if he couldn't find some way to silence her.

"You've got to take this kid home," the man at the front desk told him. "She scares away customers. She's no good for business."

Hans looked at his daughter. Her face was puffy red, and she sat before a mound of magazines, their pages crumpled and torn. "Oh, Sophie, Sophie . . ." He lifted her up, carried her outside. In his ink-stained apron, Hans waiting with Sophie for the bus to come by.

He left her in the apartment and locked the door behind him. He felt miserable back at his job. He couldn't work. He mixed the wrong chemicals, he burned the plates too long. And time passed slowly. . . . Here, where he had never watched the clock, Hans looked to see it ticking slowly: 2:00, and what seemed hours later, 2:15.

When he unlocked the door to his apartment, Hans found it cluttered and torn. "Sophie!" he called, not seeing her in the room. "Sophie!" Dishes were on the floor—some cups and plates lay broken—and the hems of the curtains were torn. Where was she? He searched frantically, imagined her fallen from the window (but how could she have opened it?).

"Sophie! SOPHIE!" In her own small room, the chest of drawers had been tipped over. He lifted it upright and found her underneath, lying face down, clutching a blue blanket.

"Oh, Sophie, Sophie, Sophie, Sophie . . ." He picked her up and she began to cry, not screaming at all, but silent rushing tears. He held her, sorry he had ever left her, promising he would never do it again, never again. It made him cry too, thinking about her, both of them alone.

She wouldn't let go of the blanket after that, a blanket he had never noticed before. Now she took it everywhere, holding it at the corner where it frayed, twirling the threads around her nose. It was tattered blue with holes, but he almost liked it. It kept her quiet, kept her company. She would lie on the bed with the blanket like a tent over her, poking her finger, a chimney, through the hole.

He wondered if she should be speaking more. Was she being too quiet for a two-year-old? Only "no" and "I want Mommy" for vocabulary?

"Blanket," he told her, pointing to her ragged companion, "Blan-ket, blan-ket," until finally she had to repeat him, "Banca," she said, "Banca," and Hans smiled, proud of his daughter.

V

He thought about taking her to a woman to be looked after, but he didn't like the idea of leaving her with someone they didn't know, all day, only to come back tired from work. It didn't seem right—not at all the way to raise one's daughter. He could quit work, but how was he to earn money? Hans thought about these things, day and night, turned them over in his mind, trying to look at all sides. He called into work, "Yes, I'm sick again, very sick, my wife and I, from goat's cheese . . . yes, another week . . . we'll recover . . . yes, I'm sure." Again he had lied, but he felt more certain this time. There were things one had to say with problems such as his, and he turned the problem over in his mind, soon forgetting the lie.

And then he realized what he should have known all along: the city was no place for his daughter. It was not a place to spend one's childhood, not at all. But the country . . . yes, things were simpler in the country. There one might not have to leave home for work. And people were kinder; one might not have to tell lies.

Now he could do nothing but build on this idea. It never left his mind. At night he couldn't sleep, and during the day he tired. They took naps on the big bed, Hans and his daughter, she and her Banca.

One night as Hans lay awake, he wondered what he was waiting for. They would leave the city—tomorrow. He had little money but enough to travel north. There was lots of land up there, where he'd grown up, and a house—the one he was born in. Hans felt it suddenly within him—the house made him sleepy by the sun—and he smelled the pine trees, the salt ocean air.

In the dark he gathered their belongings: blankets and clothing, some dishes, curtains? No, they were torn. Furniture? No, he'd have to leave the beds and chairs behind. He packed what little food they had: cans of soup, of beans, of corn, some spices? He would need those now. He would learn to cook. He would teach his daughter how.

Hans waited for the sun to streak the floor before he woke Sophie and dressed her. He tried to give her a bag to carry, but Sophie refused, letting the bag bump down the stairs. She held tightly to Banca though, as they stumbled down, he with boxes under his arms and over his shoulders. They walked through the city, and Sophie trailed Banca like a tail behind them. Hans stopped to rest his wrists and arms, then hoisted the boxes back on his shoulders. He was breathing heavily when they finally arrived at the train station.

There was a train leaving within the hour, heading northeast. Another day and they'd be in the countryside he knew but hadn't seen, hadn't seen in so long now. He wondered if anyone he knew were still living there. Some families must have stayed, not moved on to the city as he had . . .

He thought of these things as the train rumbled past where they sat waiting outside. "Train," he said, pointing to it, "train. We're going on a train, Sophie."

"GoingonatrainSophie," she said, and he smiled. She seemed happy as she kicked her legs forward, holding onto Banca, "Train, train!" she called.

At last their train arrived. Hans and Sophie boarded with their boxes. He let her sit by the window and sat down beside her.

"City," he said as they pulled out from the station, "Good-bye." Hans felt a sinking feeling as he watched the buildings blur into each other. It wasn't his any-more—the city—not the small apartment, his work. . . . But he couldn't have stayed, he thought, as the train broke into pastures of green. It wasn't his even before. But ahead . . . a blue house with white shutters, and wallpapered insides. . . . That was his house, with a trap door in the kitchen, and a basement of earth and stone underneath.

VI

They were standing in the section between cars, and Hans opened the window wide to feel the cold air rush in. Trees were speeding by; whole forests were left behind. Hans lifted Sophie to the window so she could glimpse the trees before they disappeared, and Sophie held onto Banca, letting the blanket wave bannerlike against the train.

"Banca's in the trees!" Sophie said and Hans smiled; it was her first sentence, wasn't it? But then she had let go, without meaning to, or perhaps not realizing what would happen, and the ragged blanket had gone off, settling near some tracks now far behind them.

"Where's Banca?" Sophie asked, "Where's Banca?"

Hans pulled out other blankets, but they weren't the same—large and bulky, pink, he knew that. He told her they'd find another, but she didn't listen. She stared at the window, tears streaming down her face. Hans rubbed his hands on his knees. The house ahead was his. It couldn't soothe her as it soothed him, like the place where the water met the horizon. He wanted to tell her that the blue house overlooking the sea would be her house, even more than his. Wasn't it for her they had packed their belongings into boxes?

And now she sat crying, a long and lulling cry, as if without end or beginning. Hans wondered what he could tell her, what he could give her. He had no stories or songs, only this house, "*our* house," he said to her. The rhythmic sound of the train brought them closer and closer, leaving the city far behind. In the dark he hummed the sound. Listening, Sophie soon stopped crying, losing her cry to the voice of the train.

Sometimes Hans grew scared as he sat beside his daughter, thinking: Would he have enough money? Would he have to find a job? The town had hardly any stores, and no print shop, at least it hadn't any before . . . But perhaps the town had grown. Hans imagined the dirt road paved, with a grand hospital and a bank on either side. Maybe he wouldn't need a job, wouldn't have to go into town at all. He could fish, he could garden. They could feed themselves—isn't that all they needed? And thinking of these things, of fish and sea, Hans felt calmer and looked to his daughter.

She was sitting quietly. A boy had walked up the aisle and stood before her. He smiled shyly.

"Look, Sophie," Hans said, "a playmate—don't you want to play?" But Sophie kept her eyes on the window.

Hans gave a shrug to the boy, who stood another moment, looking from Hans to his daughter, before he scampered down the aisle. It made Hans wonder: Would she have children to play with? She shouldn't be all alone. But no, he wouldn't worry, as the train rumbled forward. Soon they would arrive.

VII

The town hadn't grown. In fact, it seemed smaller than he'd remembered it. Hans didn't want to see anyone yet, wanted to get home, to their house; there were still six miles. They walked through the streets—he, weighed down with boxes; she, kicking the pebbles with the toe of her shoe. Wind skimmed the dust from the road, and Sophie rubbed her eyes as it settled on their clothes.

They walked past the old inn, past the fading grocery stand, down the road to their house. Sophie looked tired, and Hans wanted to carry her, but their boxes tugged at his shoulders and arms.

"Come, Sophie," he said, pulling her to the side of the road, "we'll wait for a car to come by." One would come, he knew, it was only a matter of waiting. Sophie scratched the dirt with a stick. Hans was showing her how to form a letter, the S in Sophie, when he recognized a distant rumbling. "Ssshh," he said, "it's coming now." He lifted her up, and they waited to see the car that made the sound.

It was Peter Hofstra. "Do you remember me?" Hans asked as he climbed inside.

Peter stared at him a moment, "I haven't seen you before," he said, turning his truck around a bend in the road.

"But I'm Hans, you knew me as a boy."

Peter turned again to stare and then laughed, "Well, so y'are. Looks like you've gone and made yourself a father." And he winked at the girl who sat in Hans' lap.

"This is Sophie, my daughter."

Peter smiled. "You got yourself a wife too, I suppose?"

Hans struggled with something inside. "My wife stayed in the city."

"She's coming out later I suppose?"

Hans nodded, thinking, he didn't have to lie, didn't have to lie at all now.

"Well, you got some visitors there in your house; they'll be surprised to see you coming along now."

"Who is it?" Hans asked, feeling his heart racing. Who could it be in his house?

"You'll see," Peter said and smiled. They were driving along the cliffs that cut down to the sea, and Hans held tightly to his daughter. He looked down to the water, a steely grey darkening in the afternoon air. He wondered if the boat would still be there, underneath the house. But his house—who was living there?

Hans saw Peter was watching him. "Ah, I'm kidding," Peter said, "there's no one there." Hans nodded, feeling his grip loosen from his daughter, and thought the water looked calm today, hardly rough at all.

"Who else lives here?" Hans asked.

"Oh, not so many; there's me and Cattie. Then let's see, Laurens and Ata . . . I don't see too much of them. I'd say they just stay inside their rickety barn. 'Course everyone else's moved on into town, or down to the city. And this is the first I heard of someone coming back." Peter looked at Hans and smiled.

They had passed Peter's house. He was taking them to the end of the road. There were just two more bends now, Hans counted, before the dirt stopped and the grass and trees took over.

"Now you come visit Cattie and me. She'll be wanting to see you and the little one," Peter said as he pinched Sophie's round cheek. Sophie looked the other way. "She's a quiet one," he said, and Hans nodded and thanked him for the ride.

The blue paint had faded and peeled from the outside. Some shutters had fallen and others dangled from rusted hinges. Hans held Sophie's hand as he pushed the door open and stepped inside.

There was brokenness all around them as they stood to the right of the door. The wallpaper hung in patches where it had torn, and shards of glass and rusted cans littered the broken floorboards. Hans felt his eyes blur, his heart beat up inside him as they walked through the kitchen with its rusted fixtures, crooked table and broken chairs into the room that had been his own as a boy.

A bearded man and a woman with long straight hair lay watching them from a mattress in the corner. "Mommy, look! Mommy!" Sophie called and ran to the bed to climb in between them. The woman reached for her, laughing, and Hans saw that she was naked under the blanket.

"Stop!" Hans called, "you can't, she's my daughter," but the woman was already holding Sophie in her arms, whispering softly in her ear, a name that wasn't hers.

"Sophie," he called, "Sophie, come back here," but Sophie was smiling, laughing as the woman rocked her back and forth, while the man looked on, taking in the both of them with his eyes. Hans stood over them, clenching his fists at his sides.

"Who are you? What are you doing here?" the man asked him.

"I'm Hans, this is my house, I'm her father . . ." Hans said loudly, but the man had turned back to the woman and child and didn't seem to have heard him.

Close Your Eyes

"Close your eyes," he said. "I want you to imagine yourself as a child. You're four years old now."

Why did they always send her back to childhood? As if it carried some mystical magic to transport her, to solve everything. If she was stuck in her life, then she was stuck, and how was anything from her childhood going to help her?

"Close your eyes," he said. "You must get rid of the past. Focus on this moment, this room, your breathing, the sounds . . ."

How did one get rid of one's past? How did one sink into oneself, discard all that came before, focus on now? Only now: the soft cushions one's bottom sunk down into, the sounds of cars streaming by, the smell of coffee . . . an electronic beeping sound threatened to unhinge her.

"Close your eyes," he said. "Now . . . follow me. Oh, stay where you are, but imagine you're walking behind me."

Why must it be *behind*—couldn't it be *beside*? Why must she have a view of his backside?

"As I step, so shall you. We are entering a forest; there are trees, we are walking along a narrow path, a bed of pine needles. The trees are spindly, it's true, an animal is watching us, do you see? What is it you see?

A cat, feral most likely, scrawny and grey with yellow eyes. Once long ago on a train in Spain, a man had told her she had *ojos de gata*, cat eyes. He seemed scared of her, mesmerized. She no longer had that power, she knew.

"What do you see?" he repeated.

"A cat, skinny, grey, maybe feral . . ."

"Ah . . . We must keep walking. The cat will follow behind us. Now we're approaching a body of water. What is it?"

"A swamp," she said. No doubt about it. And they were sinking. There were boards to walk to keep one from being sucked into the muck, but the boards themselves were sinking from their weight.

"Ah, a swamp," he repeated. "Well we must make our way through it. Soon we see evidence of a building, a house perhaps. What kind of house is it?"

What did he want her to say? That it was cozy blue with white trim, smoke drifting lazily from its stone chimney? It was a shack of course, the size of an outhouse, the roof half sunk in, the door hanging by one hinge. Filled with debris, layers of old newspapers, rusted tin cans, it was a picture of refuse. Abandoned and rotting. She was tempted to walk in, to pick through the piles, to look for . . . she didn't know what. She made her way to the door.

"You must stay behind me," he said, "we need to keep walking. Up ahead just a little farther—we're coming to a wall . . . what is it? And how high?"

A wall . . . one would say stone of course. What other option was there? In the woods? Brick? Unlikely. Cinder blocks? A row of hedges or a tangle of prickers . . .

"It's stone," she said.

"Ah . . . and is it high? Can one find its way over it?"

"Yes, I think so . . ."

"And what lies beyond?"

"Green grass, a meadow."

"Ah," he said, "That's it. We're done. I shall leave you here. You've mounted the obstacles, you've come out on the other side of them, you've—but wait . . . across the meadow, what is it?"

"It's the grey cat," she said. "It must've got ahead of us."

"Oh." He seemed disappointed. He would think of a way to turn the grey feral animal into something hopeful for her. He always did. Why did he bother?

She'd given up long ago. But he hadn't. He believed . . . it was endearing, she supposed, though frustrating, and too often like a dream, the sort of dream that keeps recurring, hardly changed and unsettling, if only for its sameness, again and again.

IV
Little Bitches

More Than Winter or Spring

I

"Do you love me more than winter?"

I see the snow, so many feet of it, high enough to jump from a building's second story and plunge down into. I feel the cold on my hands and cheeks. Ice scrapes my face.

"Do you?"

I nod my head.

"Say it then. Say it."

"I love you more than winter."

"Do you love me more than spring?"

Spring? Mud oozed between toes, walking in tractor tracks, mud thawing, trickles of ice melting . . .

"Than spring?"

I swallow, swallow spring. I hold it down, away from Jenny's prying.

"Do you?"

Jenny's voice, icicle winter voice, sticks in my throat. She leans against me, her face on mine. Eyes search it out of me. I hold my spring, unmelting inside. Now her body presses fully against mine. The warmness melts inside me. "More than spring." She's breathed it out of me.

"I love you more than summer," she whispers, "more than all the seasons combined."

II

"Jenny, what if our parents die?"

"I told you. We'd take care of each other. We could live in my house."

"Not *your* house; it smells like kitty litter.

"Well I don't like your house either. I don't like your father."

"But my father would be dead . . ."

"I still don't like your house."

"Maybe we could live somewhere else—in the woods, in a tree, a tree house. But in the winter it'd be cold . . . And what about your brother? We'd have to take care of him too. We'd need a bigger house, maybe we'd have to live in my house after all."

"You're silly. They wouldn't let us anyway."

"Who wouldn't?"

"The government. They'd put us in a place for children without parents. And we'd have to eat green beans out of cans and canned fruit at every meal and you'd have to eat canned spinach even though you hate it."

"But you said . . ."

Jenny smiles, "I was just kidding."

"You never tell the truth. You always lie."

We're walking past the huge fir tree, halfway between my house and hers. It's the Liar Tree—I named it, but I haven't told Jenny. There are things I keep knotted inside: this fir tree with its bed of needles, turned brown and soft, is my secret. I lay down on them once, underneath where branches swoop down, it's like a tent inside. They pricked my skin, a little. I felt them on my face. I cried into them, not loud enough to be heard, not loud at all. I cried because I hate Jenny's lies.

"I don't lie. You're just gullible."

"I'm not gullible!" I'm not that ugly word. I didn't know what it meant at first. I had to take the dictionary off the shelf in Father's study room, turn the pages under "G," saying it all the while: Gull-a-bull, gull-a-bull, until at last I found it, in the space after *gullet*. I hate the way it sounds: like bowls and gullies, guppies and bullies, gurgling and bubbling.

"I'm not gullible!" I shout at her and Jenny laughs. I run up the hill and she runs after me. She grabs me by the arm, and twisting it, tries to push me to the ground. I squirm, struggling. Don't want to feel the hardness melting. I wriggle from her and begin to run. My feet pound the ground, shooting new words through me. My heart throbs in my throat. When I reach the top of the hill I shout: "I HATE YOU JENNY!" hurling the words like rocks down the hill toward her.

Mother tells me to take a bath. She runs the water for me. I feel the words, branding my insides. I feel their strength, pelting through me. I let my mother hear them.

Mother laughs. "Silly girl," she says. "You're too young to know what hate is."

The next morning Jenny calls me on the phone. "Alissa, will you come play at my house?"

I remember yesterday. How I'd promised I'd never play with her again. But Jenny is my only friend. I run down the hill to her house. When I pass the Liar Tree, I close my eyes.

III

"Which would you rather?" Jenny whispers from the other bed; she's spending the night in my room. "Which would you rather: fall from a skyscraper or have to eat a whole pot of spaghetti?"

I'm falling down into darkness; I'm on my back going down. I try to lower my feet, to land feet-first, but I tumble backwards. It's like being underwater. I wonder when I'll hit the concrete of the sidewalk, and if my head will hit first, and if it does—will it crack open? Once I saw a girl run under a swing while a boy was swinging. When he swung back, the metal hit her head and all her hair got bloody. She began to scream and wouldn't stop.

"Which would you rather?" Jenny whispers again.

I start to eat the spaghetti. Just looking at the huge pot makes me feel sick, but when I take a bite, it's worse. I pull one strand and it keeps on coming. The long noodles are all connected, like the worms Jenny and I once trapped in the hole of a cinder block. They wriggled and climbed over one another, trying to escape.

"Fall from a skyscraper," I tell her. I can't eat the spaghetti. It would make me die.

"You would? But you'd die for sure that way. I'd rather eat the spaghetti. Know why?"

"Why?'

"Because you wouldn't have to eat it all at once."

"But you said—"

"I never said you had to. C'mon, your turn."

"Which would you rather: freeze to death or burn to death?" It's the hardest choice I can think of. I think about it a lot. Sometimes I think I'd rather burn, and sometimes burning seems like it must be the worst. It'd take so long to die: first your skin would turn black and crisp, then it would crinkle, and then all skinned like that, the flames would start to lick your insides, cooking them like meat. You'd be so hot and thirsty, you'd ask for water like Christ did when he was crucified. Only no one would hear you.

"I'd rather burn," Jenny whispers.

"Oh no, burning's awful!"

"But I don't want to turn into ice. I'd rather be burned."

"But if you *froze* to death, you'd turn numb and then you wouldn't feel anything!"

"I don't care. I still say *burn*."

"Freeze."

"Burn."

"Freeze! Freeze freeze freeze!"

"Burn burn burn!"

"Freeze freeze freeze freeze freeze!"

"Freeze, I mean burn!"

"Ha! You said it, you said *freeze*!"

"No-oo I didn't!"

"Did so."

"Did not!"

"Did so!"

"Okay you two, it's time to go to sleep." My father stands in the doorway.

"We can't sleep," Jenny says.

"You haven't been trying. Now go to sleep. I don't want to hear another peep out of you." He closes the door.

"Peep," Jenny says in a tiny voice and we both laugh.

IV

In Jenny's house we sleep in sleeping bags on the living room floor. We keep the window open so night comes in, and it's like we're sleeping outside. We're going to go exploring later on.

I wake up before she does. "Jenny, Jenny . . ."

"What? What's the matter?"

"It's time to go outside, remember?"

She sits up quickly. I pull my sweater over my nightgown and look around for my shoes. Jenny stuffs her pillow into her sleeping bag so it looks like someone's in it. I do the same to mine. We climb through the window and step into darkness.

I hold onto Jenny's arm. The street lamp shines down on us, pulling our shadows across the road. We keep to the edge of the hill were the trees are, so no one will see us. Behind us, houses are dark and locked up. It is our hill now. Sleeping, everyone else is dead. We hold hands as we walk up the hill, quietly, solemnly. I want it to last forever: the darkness, the sound of crickets, the breeze in the skirt of my nightgown, cold on my bare legs.

My house sits on the crest of the hill. There's a light on in one of the windows. It's my father's study room. "Jenny, look . . . my father's awake."

"Maybe we can spy on him."

We climb the tree near my house. My nightgown catches on a branch as we climb and I have to rip it to get it free. At the highest branch, his window is still too far to see into.

"I wonder why he's awake . . . He must know we're up."

"How could he know?"

"Because he does. He finds out things."

"Maybe my parents know too . . ."

We climb down the tree and run the length of the hill. But Jenny's house is dark, her parents still asleep. Inside we pull off our shoes. I crawl into my sleeping bag and try to sleep. I can still see my father's window, the only light in our house, the only light on the hill. How can he know so many things, and our secrets too?

"Jenny . . ."

She doesn't answer me.

"Jenny . . ." I know she isn't asleep. She's just pretending to be. I burrow to the bottom of my bag, down where it's dark, where no light shines through. I close my eyes and listen to things, soft things. I put my ear to them, like the belly of Jenny's cat, and listening, fall down into darkness, down into sleep.

V

Father says there is no God.

Mother says yes there is, but he's not a person, not like in pictures, but something inside ourselves.

Jenny says she isn't sure, but she knows how to find out.

We have to walk down to the cornfield, where you can see lots of sky. The cornstalks are high and we have to cut a path in between them. From here you can hardly see anything at all: just dirt, the green leaves on the stalks of corn and their heavy ears, some are bent down and in the way. We come here to play hide-and-seek with Timmy, Jenny's brother. In the cornstalks, no one can find you. But usually Timmy starts crying and ruins the game. Once Jenny and I left him hiding there, waiting for us to find him. We didn't go get him, we ran away instead. And then he started to howl, you could hear him all the way down the road. We thought the police might hear too and come find us, so we went back. Jenny called him a crybaby and Timmy said he'd tell on us. My father would've spanked us if he found out, but Jenny's parents don't believe in spanking.

This time it's different. Timmy's not with us and it's not a game—it's serious. Jenny tells me what to do.

"We have to yell real loud, all the swears you can think of. If there's a God, he'll punish us for sure, and if there isn't . . . well, nothing will happen."

I look up at the sky. A thin layer of clouds covers the blue, except where it's broken and the sky pokes through. It looks as if someone has pulled and stretched the clouds, like they were too short to cover the sky. Mother calls it Trout Sky. She thinks they look like fish scales. She says Trout Sky means tomorrow it will rain. Cornstalks must look small from way up there. Cornstalks couldn't hide us from God.

"It's gonna rain tomorrow . . ."

"Who cares? C'mon, I'm counting to three: *One . . . Two . . . Three . . .*"

"Fuck you, God!" we scream.

"Louder," she whispers, "with all your might . . ."

"FUCK YOU, GOD!"

"Damn you!" I yell, just like my father says. And then we get braver, "Go to hell, God! We know you don't exist! You're nothing, you're a shit, you're a . . . sissy!"

And then we wait. We crouch in between the stalks on our hands and knees, waiting for thunder, or lightning, or drops of rain. Or maybe God will send down words, to sting our backs, our bent shoulders. Maybe he'll burn our swears onto us and our parents will read them, when they give us baths, when they put us to bed, and everyone will know—already I feel the sting.

But no sound comes.

I raise my head to look up at the sky, to see if the clouds have shifted pattern, if they've parted, if something shines down from inside . . .

But the sky is still Trout Sky. Nothing has changed.

"Hah!" I laugh, and Jenny laughs with me. We jump up and start to dance, weaving our way through the stalks.

> *God is dead.*
> *That's what I said.*
> *He doesn't exist.*
> *He's on the shit list.*

Chanting, we swing our arms as we run down the road. We're laughing as we fall onto the grass. We roll onto our backs, our stomachs. I feel the earth under me, moving, now tilting; I close my eyes. I feel Jenny beside me and we are sliding off the earth.

Little Bitches

In those days I would wrap myself up in someone else's personality, a set of clothes that I not only tried on but wore, as if I had none of my own—I did but they didn't yet fit; I was lost in the folds or I was too bound, or the colors weren't right: too faded, mismatched—I preferred someone else's.

I don't remember how I found her. She had a boy's name and this in itself was not easily explained. There was an explanation, of course, but it didn't make sense to me then—a made-up one would have done better—something to do with a whim of her mom's (she had no father that she knew). She was not Stephanie, but Stevan.

Her breasts and hips were large like a grown woman's, not those of a nineteen-year-old, which is how old we were. She walked with a limp, as if she had a problem with her hips, as if she were already much older, thirty-five or more. And perhaps that was why I liked her. If you're trying on someone else's personality, why choose one that is—like your own—unformed?

We might have met in Spanish class. She would have been there for the credits; she already spoke almost fluently. She had lived for a time in Peru and had come back with stomach pains that were chronic. My own body was light and strong, not the always somewhat overweight self I am now. I had the elasticity of a nineteen-year-old and all the feelings of invincibility that go along with that age too. I didn't understand Stevan's pain, except that as a child my older sister had suffered from migraines—a concept I could barely begin to imagine: pain in the head—where did it come from and how did it stay there? Stevan spent what seemed like hours in the bathroom stall, groaning, complaining, while I waited for her patiently outside. I made an effort to constantly remind myself she was in pain, even to imagine what it felt like: I wouldn't remember it otherwise. Living with physical ailments was a foreign concept. But I had sympathy to spend on my friends.

Stevan was having an affair with our history professor, and this of course added to her allure. Professor Scheip was not physically attractive (pale, skinny with glasses), but he was older, and a Marxist, and he wanted her. More extraordinary even, it seemed to me, was that after two months it was Stevan, not the professor, who ended the affair. There were phone calls and notes (some of which I had to deliver to her) from him still—he wasn't ready to give it up, but Stevan was; she told me she was bored.

What did she see in me? I was solid where she slipped, could help her up when we walked the icy pavement on the midwestern campus where we went to school. While I had four brothers and sisters, she had none; while I had two parents still very much alive, she had only one: her mother who called her daily to complain about her own aches and pains and to discuss her newest live-in boyfriend. I thought those calls both a burden and an extraordinary thing—I who had to share my mother with four others, rarely got a call from Mom. It should be an emergency to spend such time and money.

For Stevan I was reassuringly normal, and I let myself be that for her. Even then I knew I was not, or I would not have had such a friend at all. I would have spent my time at the library, writing my reports and papers, drinking beer in the Rathskeller, instead of lying on a bed next to Stevan, discussing her love affair with Fidel Castro, helping her to construct it, imagining how they'd spend a day together.

Did I have obsessions of my own? I let them all be hers; I swallowed them gladly with her, like the maté she always drank, bitter and strong; we drank thermos after thermos of maté until we were just as wired, surely more so, than our classmates who lived on coffee.

We would make plans but we never went through with them. We were going to hitchhike into town, have an adventure. I'd be up and ready at 7:00 A.M., go to her room to meet her, and find her still in bed, moaning about her mysterious stomach ailments.

"*Tengo bichos*," she would tell me, those invisible Spanish bugs she'd acquired in Peru that sounded like little bitches, and I guess they were that to her: her little bitches.

Or I'd meet her in her room at night—we were going to spy on Professor Scheip with his new girlfriend, but again she was in bed, "I can't do it tonight. Let's go tomorrow, *tengo bichos* . . ."

"But we can't tomorrow—it's Sunday night! They won't be going out!"

"But I'm sick . . . I feel awful . . . *mis bichos* . . ."

Eventually I tired of the lack of adventure: the promised outings, the inevitable let-down. And then quite suddenly Stevan had to take a leave of absence. Her mother was sick; there wasn't enough money to keep Stevan in school. She was going to have to go back to California . . . I was sorry she was leaving, but our friendship also seemed to have run its course. The adventures never transpired; I was bored with Fidel Castro (Besides: hadn't she heard about how he treated political prisoners? That his island wasn't the rosy place she thought it was?). Nothing could smear her dear Fidel, dear Fidel, she would be loyal to him forever, they would meet in Habana when she slipped unseen into his mansion . . . "*Querida mia, donde has estado toda mi vida?*" Where have you been all my life, my dear?

Of course I did miss her when she was gone; there was no one else quite like her. Gone, Stevan went back to her old allure, though stronger; the patina surrounding her grew darker and more mysterious. She became the friend no one else came close to; it was never "Stevan," but always "My friend Stevan," as if she occupied a sacred corner no one else could enter.

But gradually our letters, never very frequent, dwindled to nothing. The temporary leave of absence became permanent. I made other friends, even had a boyfriend for a while; graduated, I moved to San Francisco. I got a job in a bookstore in the Mission District, a store with well-stocked Latin American and political science sections. It was a homey place, with next-to-no pay but friendly fellow workers and customers.

One day while I was trying to fix the broken coffee pot (we always had a pot of coffee on for customers to help themselves to), a voice interrupted me.

"Is that coffee ready yet?"

I glanced up and knew immediately it was she. She had changed so little; her ribbed sweater and tight jeans showing off her curves, her black hair still loose and long. My own hair was cut short like a boy's, a lock over my forehead; perhaps that was why she didn't recognize me.

"Stevan," I said, and she looked at me, startled. "It's Callie."

The look-over she gave me was long and steady, appraising my clothes, taking in my every gesture. And then she hugged me. She was strong and warm; I could feel her wide hips and her full breasts against my smaller ones. "I'm so glad," she said, "I knew I would find you."

We caught ourselves up on each other's doings: Stevan was helping refugees from El Salvador get settled into the Bay Area; it was a new program, one she had helped get started. I had roommates while she had none; she'd worked hard since leaving college, had saved her money and could afford her own place, albeit a very small one, downtown.

We made plans. I would meet her Sunday morning (my next day off) at her apartment at 10 A.M., then we'd take the boat to Alcatraz, have a picnic.

Sunday morning was cool, almost cold—I was always surprised that San Francisco wasn't warmer. Scraps of paper flew against me as a gust of wind suddenly blew through the street, empty of strollers and midweek traffic. I passed a brick building with narrow slits for windows, an old fortress or prison. I scanned numbers for her address. Places were boarded-up, closed; nothing looked even remotely like an apartment. At last I found it: a glass door, 324 above it. Stevan had told me to ring the buzzer, but when I tried the door, it opened. I walked up to the third floor, knocked on #5.

"Who is it?" I heard.

"Me, Callie," I answered. I waited for her to respond, to open the door. I knocked again. Finally I turned the handle and went in.

She was sitting in bed, a flimsy pink negligee barely covering her. She held a gun in both hands; it was pointing straight at me.

"Stevan! What are you doing?"

"Oh, it's you," she said, putting the gun down on the pillow beside her. "Well, you never know. . ."

"Just who were you expecting?" My eyes were on the gun resting on her pillow. Was it cocked and loaded? What if she'd pulled the trigger?

"Oh, god knows . . .this place is bugged—I'm followed all the time now."

"By who?"

She gave a look, one she used to give me when we were in college: don't be so stupid, don't you know anything? "Who do you think? The FBI. They've got my phone bugged. They follow me everywhere—one of these days . . ."

I wanted her to put the gun away. I hated that it was so near where she was. At the same time I couldn't stop staring at her. I could see her breasts through the filmy nightgown; they were pear-shaped, large but somehow delicate, full and loose under her ridiculous nightdress.

"Stop staring and sit down," she said. "Here, sit on the bed."

She patted a place for me. There was nowhere else to sit. She had no armchair or couch in the room. Only the bed, a standing lamp, an eat-in kitchen in the far corner.

"Sit down," she said again, "C'mon, sit beside me."

I did as she said, and again my eyes didn't know where to rest: on the gun, or her smooth face, her hazel eyes, the way her breasts were elongated while her dark nipples stood out, brushing against the sheer fabric.

"How are you? I've thought about you so many times . . . I'm sorry I stopped writing . . ."

"Are you still in love with Fidel Castro?" I blurted. Where had that come from? A stupid question, but it was what came to me, as if there were nothing else more urgent.

"*Ah Fidel . . .*" she laughed. "*Mi Fidel.* Of course I am. *Soy fiel a Fidel . . .* ," she liked how it rhymed, I'm faithful to Fidel. "But I have a real boyfriend now—Julio. From El Salvador. He's the best." She smiled at me. "And you? Any boyfriends?"

I shook my head. I could feel my face reddening. "I had a boyfriend," I said, "but . . ."

"But what?"

"Nothing, it wasn't serious." My face was burning. Why didn't she put some clothes on?

"Stevan . . . ," I said, and she looked at me, waiting. I saw the slope of her shoulder, her slightly tanned skin. Her breasts hung and quivered. "Can you put that gun away? It's making me nervous."

"Oh, this," she said, picking it up off the pillow. "I'd forgotten all about it. Here," she said, handing it to me, "You want to see how it feels?"

"Not especially," I said, my voice suddenly back with me.

"Here, feel it. It's not as heavy as you'd think. Take it," and she thrust it toward me. I'd never held a real gun. It had a solid feel, smoothly polished. I stood up with it. I was afraid to touch anything on it, to press something into action. I carried it into the kitchen.

"Hey, where are you taking my baby?"

I opened a drawer next to the sink, placed it in there.

"Hey, Callie . . . Come back here."

Stevan had gotten out of bed. Her nightgown had a pink ruffle that fell just below her bottom. Where had she ever bought such a thing? "Come on back here," she said and she led me to her bed.

"Stevan, aren't we going to Alcatraz? Aren't you going to get dressed?"

"Oh, sure. Why not? I just move slow in the morning. You were always faster," and she laughed, as if she'd made a joke, a double entendre I was missing.

It occurred to me she was drunk, that she'd been drinking. Why else was she moving so slowly, languorously, acting so absurdly?

"You forgot, Callie. You forgot about *mis bichos* . . ." and she laughed again and then sighed. "Let's just lie down a little, I'm not feeling so wonderfully. You never did realize, did you? About my illness?"

I didn't know anymore what she was talking about, what she was saying to me. She lay down on the bed and told me to lie beside her. A strand of her dark hair fell against my face and it smelled sweet to me, lightly perfumed. She kept talking to me, slipping in and out of Spanish, while at the same time, pulling me closer, her arm around my shoulder. She let my head rest between her breasts, soft and fleshy, undoing the tie on her nightdress, so that the halves parted and I saw how close her nipple was, and wondered how it might taste and felt my tongue licking a path along her tanned skin toward it. I moved so slowly and quietly I was barely aware myself of my movements.

And from this gentle slowness, I emerged, fevered and hungry, so deeply hungry that the voice inside me—But I'm making love with a woman—what am I doing?—was easily squashed, had no life of its own, no life at all. She undid my buttons and zippers, helped to pull all my cumbersome clothing off me, and soon I felt the full warmth of her body against mine and wanted to leave none of it untouched or untasted.

"Well, Callie," she said, having stood up and dressed finally, in a billowy-feminine blouse and pants, "I always knew you were gay." She looked at me and laughed, and her laughter may have been warm, but to me it felt harsh, judgmental.

"What do you mean? What are you talking about?"

"What I said: I always knew, that's all."

She was standing in the middle of her room now, combing her hair out from her head in that peculiar way she had, bending from the waist down and brushing it out from the roots.

"How did you know? And what about you?"

"Me?" she said. She was applying lipstick now, twisting her lips as she stared at her reflection in the mirror against the wall. I had started to grab my clothes and put them back on; I suddenly felt cold, self-conscious. "Oh, I could never be gay. I love dicks too much for that," and she turned to me and gave me a fully-rouged lipstick smile.

"But what about what just happened? What about that?"

"It was very nice," she said, and she came over and kissed me lightly on my forehead, leaving a red smudge, I knew. "It was really nice, but it just happened, that's all. It happened once . . . I'm not gay."

"And you think I am?"

She smiled again. "Don't you know it," she said softly.

I suddenly hated her. I hated her for her rouged lips, her wide hips, for her stomach pains and her condescension. I saw that I'd hated her all along, had hated her in college and when she went away, hated her when I saw her in the bookstore—I had always hated Stevan—why couldn't I have seen that? I went to the sink and washed my hands and face, combed my hair back into place.

She had gone into the bathroom, closed the door shut. I suddenly remembered the gun. I had an image of Stevan emerging from the bathroom and me pointing the gun straight at her—just as she'd done earlier to me, only I'd pull the trigger. . . . I opened the drawer; it was sitting just as I'd left it. My heart was beating loudly, and I saw as I reached for it that my hand was shaking. I closed my hand around it, shut the drawer very carefully, then carried the gun to where my knapsack was resting. I took out the extra sweater I'd brought and wrapped the gun inside it. I stuffed the whole thing back in.

I felt odd, jittery, yet strangely sure of myself. I who'd always hated guns, who as a child was never allowed to play with them, who couldn't be more weapons-ignorant—I didn't even know what kind it was. A pistol surely.

"Stevan," I knocked on the bathroom door, "I'm going."

"What? You can't go . . . why are you leaving? You can't go now," she repeated.

"I'm going," I said again, "Good-bye."

"But Callie . . ." she protested.

I didn't stay to hear the rest. I knew it would feel like hours before she emerged from the bathroom. I wasn't going to wait for her.

My heart was loose in my chest as I walked, then ran from her apartment. Cars drove by, too slowly it seemed, and I nearly bumped into the woman and her dog who walked past me.

I wasn't myself. Surely anyone could see that—there was something different about me. They must all know that: that I'd stolen a gun, that I was part criminal. All I had to do now was complete the picture.

I didn't know where I was headed; I only knew I wasn't going to my apartment. Images came intermittently, stayed too long: climbing to the roof of a building, pointing the gun at anyone who walked under me. Or I'd hide behind the corner of the next building, shoot the first unlucky person to step in front of me. Most often I saw myself hiding out across the street from Stevan's building, waiting for her to emerge, then holding the gun in two hands, feet planted . . . Always my aim was deadly.

I walked city streets, headed uphill, eventually getting to where you had a view of Twin Peaks. I covered all the streets in the neighborhood below. Too tired to walk farther, I got on a bus and took it to the last stop. A light drizzle had started to fall, and I was shivering, but still I wouldn't open my knapsack, take out my sweater.

I couldn't go back to my apartment. I told myself I couldn't risk my roommates finding it, but it was really myself I was afraid of. I carried it on my back, wondering what I was going to do with it.

I got on another bus, one that went out past the park, then through the fogged-in neighborhood of Richmond. I got out and walked past houses, each with its requisite lawn patch; in the mist everything looked the same to me. I crossed the highway, letting cars speed past me.

It wasn't like a deep rushing river—what had I been thinking? Why wasn't anything presenting itself as the neatest, cleanest solution? But my mind felt numb, incapable of its usual workings; I was cold and shivering. I walked along the beach, away from the sound of traffic, closer to the ocean. I waited until I felt sure no one was watching (but who could see anything in the thick fog?), then unwrapped it from its sweater-nest. I hurled it as far as I could into the ocean.

My pitch had never been terrific. I knew it would sink to the bottom though, and from there it might get covered in tide-shifting sands, become encrusted with salt—in time, even barnacles.

I went back to my apartment and spent the next day, the last before I had to go back to work, in bed.

I sometimes wondered: if I hadn't stolen the gun, would Stevan and I still be friends? Lovers even? She knew I had taken it, called me in my apartment to demand where it was, to convince and cajole me, and when that didn't work, to threaten me. Didn't I realize what I'd done? What it was I'd taken from her? She was being followed, her phone was bugged, even now they were listening in . . . She needed it—couldn't I get that through my thick head? I had better return it, I had to, she had to have it, surely even an idiot could understand that. She was going to search my apartment, she was sending her boyfriend after me.

For a while the phone calls were a constant. I even got used to them. In a strange way, I almost looked forward to them. I always denied that I had taken the gun: I didn't take it. I have no idea where it is. Maybe your boyfriend stole it. You're wasting your time. I never touched it.

That was all I ever said: I didn't take it, and she must have grown bored with the response, because finally the phone calls stopped, and even though I sometimes tried—straying too close to her neighborhood, once even walking by her apartment—I didn't run into her again. Years later in a distant city, I would again—but by then she'd forgotten. Her inability to remember, her insistence that no such thing had ever transpired was so confident, so complete, that for a long time I had to wonder if it wasn't I who'd been half-crazy.

Waiting

He comes into the café, eyes peering over his glasses, obviously in search of someone. And then because I am sitting with only time in front of me—

Are you—?

I nod. He hasn't said a name, so no lie has been spoken.

He looks relieved. He slides into the seat in front of me, the other half of my booth. It's my favorite seat in the café, one I often have to wait for, settling for a loose table somewhere in the meantime.

Ah . . . he says. Well, shall we . . .?

Mmmm, I nod.

He isn't good-looking. He's overweight and aging—I wonder why I've allowed myself to be taken in by him (but isn't it the other way around, he is my own victim?)

I think I'll start with coffee, he says.

Yes, by all means, I tell him.

Would you like anything—?

I smile at him. I'll have another coffee.

I watch him wait in line. He's very impatient. He keeps rocking back on his heels and trying for the waitress' attention, though there are at least four people ahead of him. I realize suddenly there's a woman probably in search of him. What did they do? Respond to each other's personals? I look around for her—a woman on the hunt for him—but I don't find her. For a moment I feel sorry for him, waiting impatiently to buy himself and me coffee. Ten years ago, he could have been my father, but I'm too old for that now. It's a shame how age spares no one. On the other hand, I've stopped celebrating birthdays. They used to be so important to me—a day for wonderful things—but I've realized it's better to ignore them. My actual number is vague to me . . . I'm in a fluid state, not counting.

He arrives with my coffee.

That was very kind of you, I offer. He can't know how much I mean that.

Well, he says. These things are awkward.

Yes, aren't they? Let's just enjoy our coffee.

He looks relieved. I wonder what my role is. I look around for the other woman, cannot place her.

It's a nice café, he offers. Do you come here often?

I don't want to reveal myself. No, it's my first time here.

Ah, me too. He smiles at me.

I begin to feel bored, impatient. I don't want to feel trapped by him. Well, I might as well let you know, I tell him, I've decided not to go through with it.

You can't mean that.

But I do.

But on the phone you said—

Yes, but I've changed my mind.

I see. But—

He wants to ask me something else, I can tell. The question is hard for him. I'm not sure what I am denying him, but I can see I've made it difficult. I do feel sorry for him, I won't pretend I don't. His hand is on the table, fingering a napkin. I place my own over his, grip his fingers. They feel soft and pudgy, younger than the rest of him. Don't feel bad, I tell him. It isn't because of you, exactly.

His eyes hold mine. I think I see water filling around the edges, but I'm not sure about that. With his glasses on, it's hard to tell. You've gone back on your promise, he says. I can't let you do that.

Even promises can be broken.

I can hear the heartlessness of my own reply. My eyes rest on the specks of dandruff on the shoulders of his suit jacket. His shirt is open at the collar; curls of greyish-white hair poke through. I sense he's recently divorced, teetering on the brink of something. Are there children in the picture?

You've disappointed me tremendously.

His voice trembles with the word *tremendously*, a tremor, a crack in the human landscape.

I gave you nothing to go on. You shouldn't have counted on me.

I don't see how you can say that.

It isn't hard.

He stares at me. The pools in his eyes seem to have steadied; if they're a well, it's full by now.

You lack humanity.

I don't see how you can say that, you barely know me.

It isn't hard, he says.

He's quoting me. That makes me want to smile, but I stop myself. Smile, and we'll be starting all over again. I want my booth back to myself. I've missed the afternoon sun, the way it comes in through the window to warm me. I wonder if I'll have to leave first to get rid of him. I don't want to have to do that.

I scoot myself out from behind the table to stand before him. I'm going to the Ladies Room. I'll say good-bye to you now, since you may decide to leave before I come out. I take his hand in a handshake, press his fingers against mine to make it heartfelt. I'm sorry it didn't work out. I did enjoy meeting you, even so.

He stares at me. He hasn't figured out what to say yet.

Now, if you'll excuse me. I try a smile on him, one that's both winning and that asks for forgiveness.

I take a long time in the Ladies Room, brushing my hair, re-applying makeup. I wash my hands and let the electric dryer dry them, down to the last bit of moisture. I like the bathroom; it's clean and spacious. There's even a changing table for mothers with babies; it's very thoughtful. And the dried flowers look new, as if the management just replaced the arrangement. It's an unusual café that has such a pleasant bathroom.

He isn't there when I come out, just as I predicted. I slide in my booth, close my eyes to the afternoon sun. It's waning. I hear the buzz of voices, people talking, too loud to make me very happy. Perhaps it's time to leave after all. The day seems to have gone by without me. I open my eyes to take in my surroundings. He hasn't left me anything. Only his napkin, twisted into a tight strand, shredded at the end.

～

Dear Dr. Haskell

12 November 2008

Dear Dr. Haskell:

I've decided to stop seeing you. What good does it do me? You can't bring my wife back. As far as I can tell, I've made no progress on the road to recovery, to reconstructing my life, a life, any life. With the exception of a substantial dent in my savings, after eight months I see no change to speak of. Instead, I'm being made to wallow. I'm sitting on the floor, stuck in a muddy puddle, and everything is the color of shit. It stinks here.

Yesterday was what did it. That dead mouse, the putrid smell . . . don't you think it would have been expedient to find another office? Borrow someone else's? The odor was so foul I couldn't concentrate. When I left your grungy excuse for an office, I felt sure it had seeped into me, polluted my clothes, my skin, my brain while it was at it. How could you go on sitting there? What on earth were you thinking?

But let's leave aside for the time being this mouse that hid itself so expertly before sacrificing itself to stink up your office. I'll get to the point here. The point is Tina. Why on earth do I need to keep talking about her? Clearly, it's for you and not me. My own feeling here is the less said, the better. The less dwelled on, the more chance of moving on. But with you, it's as if there's nothing else worth discussing. The fact that she left me for another woman only makes her more appealing.

Of course, I know you, Dr. Haskell, and you will deny this, are vociferously denying it this very moment. She is of no interest whatsoever to you except, that is, in relation to me. But in each and every session your questions betray you:

Have your heard from her?

Has she written you?

Where is she living now?

What is she doing for work?

Is her partner supporting her?

What a good story it makes after all, an intriguing case study, the kind you barely come across anymore: husband's wife of 14 years leaves him for a woman she met online and fell hard for . . .

Yesterday I stood on a bridge, the one near the power plant. The water rushed and swirled below, higher than usual from all the rain we'd had. I stared into the swirling water, I felt magnetized, mesmerized. I gripped the railing; it was all I could do to keep from being sucked in, from in one quick jump leaving it all behind me.

I'd like to put *you* under the microscope for a change, Dr. Haskell, probe and poke your tics and foibles, your murky present and recent past. Shall I address those questions you're so anxious to have answered?

1. *Have you heard from her?* Not since she left me.

2. *Has she written you?* Refer to response #1.

3. *Where is she living now?* As far as I know she's still in Berlin with her beloved lesbian-art-gallery-owner.

4. *What is she doing for work?* How should I know?

5. *Is her partner supporting her?* It seems right to assume so. After all, Tina's the one who gave up everything to truck—fly, rather—herself out there for Ms. Online-Poacher-looks-like-a-hunk-of-male-anatomy.... What the hell does Tina see in her? Good God. It's scary.

I should have known when Tina was spending so much time on the Net that it would end badly, I should have stopped her. This idea that you make friends with people in Germany, Argentina, in Indonesia for God's sake . . . well, there's nothing inherently wrong with it, of course, but the problem was that these friends of hers, these ephemeral web-beings with names like Dusty, Zoë, Fern, Nerva, and Robotics were replacing her real friends, her very real-living-close-by-would-do-anything-for-her friends . . . she stopped meeting Carrie for tea, or Jim for dinner (something I never objected to of course, though Jim being gay made it easier), we stopped having Bob and Marie over, or anyone else, for that matter. And let's not talk about what was happening in bed . . . I couldn't interest her. She'd get up at 2 A.M. to write back to Helga, because it was 7 A.M. in Berlin, and she knew Helga had woken, showered and dressed and was now drinking coffee and writing her. I suppose Helga was sitting with bathroom open, tits exposed. Tina too. They were having a fuck-fest, never mind that there were thousands of miles, oceans of country and clunky PC monitors between them . . .

And you, Dr. Haskell, think it's a turn on. That my wife's been brainwashed, corrupted, stolen, that my life's been ruined . . . well, it doesn't compare to the scintillation you feel, does it? I bet you take it to bed with you, I bet envisioning the two of them doing it in front of their PCs, or in that messy loft in Berlin, helps you get it up and keep it up, helps you satisfy yourself and your own wife too while you're at it. Well, good for you. Good for you and Helga and Tina, and good for your wife too, who's the beneficiary. Lucky for all of you, you cocksuckers, cuntlickers, sex-obsessed s/he-devils. I seem to be the only one left out of this sex festival.

Dear Dr Haskell:

I haven't thrown myself into the river.

Not yet.

But I chucked the PC Tina and I shared—not her laptop, she took that with her of course, accomplice as it was to her new romance—but the bulky Dell she and I used to take turns on until she broke her leg and wanted a laptop for use in bed and I bought her one, and that was the beginning of the end . . .

I got rid of the PC in the only way that felt real . . . I chucked it into the Housatonic. I know I was littering, but isn't the river already filled with the PCBs that G.E. used to dump in? I couldn't help it, I had to do something, and your little sit, talk and stink all occasions weren't helping. It was heavy and I couldn't park on the bridge of course, being the one lane that it is, and I couldn't risk someone seeing me, so I went at night, or at two in the morning rather, carried it in my arms like a child, the child I wanted but never got to have, I carried it to the middle of the bridge, leaned over the rail, held it there, before I dropped it to a very satisfying plunk and clunk into the rushing river below, swollen from the rains we've had.

How satisfying it felt. Sure the feeling didn't last long . . . but it felt *good*. Better than any one of your sessions ever did. I'm sure if the thing's ever found it'll be too waterlogged to reveal any incriminating evidence in my direction . . . and I know you yourself won't betray me. But who the hell cares, anyway? It's just a fucking PC. I'm not the one who abandoned my spouse of 14 years without so much as an explanation, anything that makes any sense anyway, because nothing does . . . I'm not the one who gave up on our marriage, a well-built lasting relationship, for something fleeting and trendy and sexy and silly. And I'm not the one who needs help. You are. You're a voyeur, Dr. Haskell. You're living vicariously through your patients, watching as we crawl through the tangled mess of our lives, because apparently this excruciating mess is more exciting than your own.

I've chucked the PC, Dr. Haskell.

And now I'm chucking you.

I've chucked the clothes, her makeup, her books, the paintings she left behind . . . I should've taken it to Goodwill or the Salvation Army, but I didn't want it to be recycled into the world . . . it's toxic junk. It's gone now. I burned most of it, what I could, and tossed the rest in that huge-ass dumpster at the Transfer Station.

I've stripped the house of all that belonged to her. I've even stripped the wallpaper. I'm pulling it off in large chunks, I'm inhaling the dust, I'm breathing pink and mint-green plaster dust. My snot's discolored, I'm taking it into my lungs. I'm stripping these rooms, these walls, I'm shrouded in this goddam wallpaper, strips of it hanging, my fingernails are rebelling, my cuticles torn. I've opened the windows to let in the cold

November air. I can hear the river rushing nearby, its sound is lulling, thrilling.

Violin Lessons

My fingers are little bones that do things I don't want them to. But if I tell them what to do it isn't any better. Sometimes what they do is right; they know without my telling them and I pull the bow gently along the strings and suddenly it all seems easy and I think, I can do this, it isn't hard; I'm doing it now, and Mr. Romero is smiling at me. This is it, I think, I'm going to be a great violinist, I know I am, it was hard for me, but now . . . And then the bow scrapes from pressing so hard and I can see from Mr. Romero's face that he doesn't love me anymore.

I remember the first day. It was under the Christmas tree. The case was black and inside it was velvet green. The violin was orangey-red. Amber color, Mom said. It was beautiful, shiny and delicate, and it was mine. I would open up the case, three or four times a day, just to look at it.

I loved everything about it, even the resin. It was like a golden ice cube, clear where the bow polished it again and again—the color of honey, like honey that had hardened—it made you want to put it in your mouth and suck on it. Even the scarf Mom gave me to wrap the violin in seemed special, soft and silky, with a trace of her perfume. Now it only reminds me of Mr. Romero. He wears one around his neck and tucks it into his shirt.

Mr. Romero is from another country. Mom says he's the best teacher she's ever had. She has her lesson before mine. She's smiling when she comes out and Mr. Romero is smiling too. He still has a smile when he sees me come in, but I know he won't keep it. I want him to. Maybe this time he will, I think, maybe this time I'll know exactly what to do. I pick up my violin. I bring the bow to the strings. He stops me to correct my fingers. They're too scrunched together. The pads of my fingers have to fit squarely on the strings. They can't roll on their sides. He says I don't hold the bow correctly. It's how my last teacher taught me. Mr. Romero says I can't grip it like that. It has to be loose. "Loosen! Loosen!" he says. But if I loosen my fingers, the bow will fall away from me. It bumps on the strings. I have to hold it tightly in order to play.

"No. No, no, no! Not like that! You're too violent! It's not violent. You need grace, not force. You can't force it. It's light, see, it's . . ."

He picks up the violin to show me. Of course he makes it look easy. It's true his body is loose when he plays. He sways. He doesn't stand still. The music fills him; it fills the room. Even when he stops, it stays in the room; I can hear it. "Okay?" he says. "Have you got it now?" But I know I don't. I don't have to start playing to know. I shake my head. "What do you mean?" he says. "Try it. You must try it." I fit the violin under my chin. I place my fingers on the strings. I lift the bow; I'm trying to hold it gently. Maybe I can do it after all, I think, maybe I'll get it right this time. I start the bow across the strings. It makes a little scraping sound. For a second I see him close his eyes and then I know it's over: he'll never love me again.

After the lesson I go to my room. Downstairs they're talking. He's talking to my mother about me, I know he is. "She's too violent," he's probably telling her. But what does that mean? My last teacher never said that about me. She thought I was good, maybe even very good. Once she said I was almost a natural, like Mom is. Why did she have to leave? She got married and moved to Cincinnati, wherever that is.

I look out the window—his car's still there. So he hasn't left yet. But what can they be talking about? I wish he'd leave. Go away, go away, go away . . . I start downstairs.

They're in the living room. They're sitting on the couch together. Mom's laughing about something—what could be so funny? Mr. Romero looks more handsome when he's with her than with me; he doesn't look so stern—his face is softer. He has hair that comes down past his ears, but the top of his head is balding. Before Mr. Romero, I'd never seen a grown man with long hair.

"Alissa!" Mom says. I didn't want them to see me.

"Well," he says, standing up, "It's time that I go."

"Well . . . ," my mother says.

"Now, Alissa," he says to me, "are you going to practice as I told you to?"

I nod. When he says my name, he makes it sound exotic, the s's sounding like z's.

"She's a little . . . how shall I say it? Tight . . . stiff—that's the word."

How can he say that about me? My mother puts her hand through my hair. "Well, she'll learn. We couldn't find a better teacher, could we?"

"Oh, well . . . ," Mr. Romero says.

My mother smiles at him.

"Well, then . . . ," he says.

"We'll see you next Wednesday . . ."

"Yes, on Wednesday," he says.

"You have to try a little harder," my mother says after he leaves.

"Why? What did he say?"

"You heard him . . ."

"No, before that . . ."

"What? He didn't say anything. He said . . . you have to practice more."

"More? I practice every day."

"I know you do."

"So why do I have to practice more?"

"Because . . . Do you want me to help you?" she says.

"No, I don't want you to help me . . ." I go into the kitchen and take a glass of orange juice. "I'm going outside," I yell to her from the kitchen.

I'm going over to Mrs. Vachel's. She's an artist; she did a drawing of me. She said she'd never seen a child sit so still. I sat on the couch and I didn't move; I didn't look away and I didn't scratch my nose, even though it itched, and I waited even though I had to go to the bathroom after a while. Mrs. Vachel said she'd never seen anything like it. She said she wants me to sit for her again sometime. I saw the picture. It even looked like me. Except I looked older. Mrs. Vachel said that too. Would you think that was a picture of a nine-year-old? It's because you look so serious, she said.

I knock on her door. No one comes. I'm about to go away when the door opens. "Oh, Alissa! It's you. . . . What—did you come for something?"

"I thought maybe that, um … if you were drawing…"

"Oh, is it about sitting? How nice of you to come! It's just that it's almost dark now. I prefer the morning light. . . . Could you come back on the weekend—how about Saturday? Saturday morning."

I nod to her as I back away. "Okay?" she says, "We'll see you on Saturday?"

"Okay," I yell back at her. But I know I won't come. She'll have to ask me again, if she really wants me to—why did she say she wanted me to if she really doesn't? I don't care about her anyway. She's no better than Mr. Romero.

Before Mr. Romero all the days of the week were the same to me. It didn't matter: Monday, Tuesday, Wednesday . . . Now I hate Wednesday. How could I ever think it was a nice word, a nice day? I'm always thinking about Wednesday. It seems there are more Wednesdays than ever before and they last longer than Tuesdays or Thursdays. Anyway it's a stupid word—I don't know why I didn't realize it before. You don't even write it like you say it; you have to say it differently to remember how to spell it: Wed-nes-day. Stupid. Every time it comes around again I want to stay in bed and never get up and when I walk back from school I hope something happens to me, a car stops and someone comes to take me away. I walk slowly, my feet slowing me down, but sometimes that makes it worse; I get tired and feel heavy, and I can never really forget about it anyway. But I still have some hope. Maybe he won't show up this time. Maybe he'll be sick or maybe his car will break down or maybe he'll have decided to go back to his own country. I don't understand why he left it in the first place.

My mother is waiting for me. "Alissa, what took you so long? Mr. Romero's been waiting."

He smiles at me. "How are you today?" he says.

"Fine." I look at the clock: 3:35. Why does he have to come on time? Couldn't he ever be late? I take off my coat and go into the living room to get my violin. I keep my eyes on my violin as I get the bow ready. "Be good today," I want to tell it. "Don't make me mess up . . ." Before it felt like it was on my side, but now . . . I don't feel like I can count on it, I don't know how it will behave, even though I practice almost every day.

"Let's start where we left off the other day," he says. He's looking at me eagerly, like he still likes me. Maybe he does, I think. Maybe it's not too late yet . . .

I look at the music. Why can't I play it like when I was practicing—when Mom came in and told me it sounded good? I position my fingers and look at the notes jumping across the page. I know these notes, I've learned them already . . . I bring the bow across the strings; I've started a little bit off but I keep on going, I don't look at him, just the notes, their little ant bodies hanging upside down and some right side up with their flags hoisted. I keep on going, it's not so bad I think . . .

He smiles at me. "This is good," he says. "I see you have been working hard. Now, you mustn't forget to breathe!" He shows me, his stomach going in and out, "We don't have to stop breathing when we play! We can move a little with the music, you see, we can feel it inside our bodies, you see?" He plays the same piece I did, only it sounds different when he plays it, like the music is thicker; I can feel it all around me. He half-closes his eyes; he doesn't need to read the notes. He moves into the music; I can see him going inside of it, and his long hair sways as he plays.

"I can see improvement. She's been working very hard, I think," he says to my mother when the lesson is finally over and she comes into the room.

She smiles at him. "I'm delighted," she says. "So we're not too much work for you, after all?"

He laughs. "If this is work, then let me just imagine *pleasure*—it must be heaven . . ." His dark eyes seem to sparkle when he says this. "Don't you know? I look forward to every Wednesday . . . It would be best if it were more than once a week, wouldn't it? But I understand, right now, that's not possible . . ."

I look at my mother. Is that what they were talking about?

"Well, maybe later on . . . Would you like that, Alissa?" Mom says, looking at me.

I nod. How can I say no in front of him?

They're still talking as I wrap my violin in its silk scarf, place it gently in its case and snap it closed. I put it in its place next to my mother's. Her case is different, brown with metal trim, more modern-looking. But I like my own small black one. "Thank you," I tell him before I leave the room.

"Yes, yes, I'll see you next Wednesday . . ."

I take the stairs up to my room. I can hear Mom laughing. My feet come down heavily. I step down hard on each step as their laughter fades behind me.

It happens in the next lesson. Everything I've ever learned goes white inside me.

"How many times have we been going over this? Do you know I have students who learn this in two lessons? Why is it so hard for you?"

"I don't know," I say, and I hate how my voice sounds, weak and spidery.

"What more can I do—I don't know what more I should do to teach you . . ."

His shoulders heave as he stares at me. I can see beads of sweat on his forehead. Am I really so hard for him?

"Come, let us try once more . . ."

I bring the violin to my shoulder again, position my fingers very carefully, start the bow across the strings. But I know this is the end. It was only luck before; I'll never get it back again. I play, without any hope I play the piece for him, knowing it's all over, I keep on, until suddenly he interrupts me, "What, what, what are you doing? What is this? Tell me, please, what is this, this—this is not *music*, no, this is something different entirely . . ."

I don't look at him. I don't want him to see that I'm going to cry, but the tears are already filling my eyes, running slowly down. I put my violin in its case—I don't even loosen the bow—and snap it closed. I place the case next to my mother's, her new brown one. I don't turn back to look at him as I leave the room.

"Alissa, please . . .what is happening? I didn't mean for—please . . .tell me . . ."

I keep on walking. I don't say anything. Once through the double doors I run up the stairs to my room. I throw myself on the bed and bury my face in the pillow. Go to hell, I think, and watch him marching down to hell. Dad used to say there was no hell. No heaven or hell, just the ground you get buried in when you die. But I decide not to believe him. Why should I believe him now? I send Mr. Romero down. It's so hot he wants to turn back, but the devil's behind him. Laughing. Soon the tips of his hair, his long fuzzy black hair, catch on fire.

By the time my mother comes up to the room, both Mr. Romero and my violin are dead—burnt and splintered. I've smashed my violin into a million tiny pieces. I stood on my bed to jump on it with a mighty leap: Crunch. One more jump and the whole body of it is in smithereens. Smithereens. Everywhere. Everything but the neck. The neck won't break but the body does.

"Alissa, what happened? Mr. Romero feels terrible."

Mom has sat down on the bed beside me.

"Can you tell me? Can you explain it please? Mr. Romero doesn't understand what he did . . ."

Why does she keep talking about *him*? I roll over to face the wall. I might have told her, I might have tried to explain to her, but it seems impossible now. She sits on the bed a long time without me answering. I lie still. I can see the face I always see on the wall near my pillow. Sometimes I think it won't be there again—it took so long for me to see that it *was* a face and not a brown smudge. But once you see it, once you notice the hooked nose and chin—the old man's face in a profile—you always see it, every time. It's never gone away, not since I finally noticed it.

"Alissa, can't you tell me anything? What upset you? Was it something he said? Can you tell me? Please?"

I don't say anything. I don't move, even when I breathe. Nothing moves. Even Mom beside me isn't moving or touching me. I think about Mrs. Vachel. "Unnaturally still," I heard her say about me. I wish she were going to paint me because I'm not going to move, I'm not going to speak, I'm going to stay like this forever, not violent or forceful, but silent and unmoving, better than anyone else has ever done.

Acknowledgments

Many thanks to the editors of the following print and online journals in which these stories first appeared: *American Literary Review, Boston Fiction Review, The Brooklyn Rail, Double Room, Gargoyle, Lake Affect, Outsider Ink, Pennsylvania English, Quarterly West, Red Brick Review, San Miguel Writer, Slipstream,* and *3rd Bed.*

Thanks are due to the editors of the following anthologies which also included a number of these stories: *Wild Cards: The Second Virago Anthology of Writing Women* (Virago Press, UK), *PP/FF: An Anthology* (Starcherone Press), *Wreckage of Reason: An Anthology of Contemporary Xxperimental Prose by Women Writers* (Spuyten Duyvil), *An Intricate Weave: Women Write about Girls and Girlhood* (Iris Ed.), *The Nine Muses* (Wheatland Press), and *You Have Time for This: Contemporary American Short-Short Stories* (Ooligan Press).

The only thing one can give an artist is leisure in which to work. To give an artist leisure is actually to take part in his creation. —Ezra Pound

For granting me a residency and the leisure in which to work at Civitella Ranieri in Umbertide, I am grateful to the Civitella Ranieri Foundation. Thanks also to Dr. Barbara Douglass and Northwestern Connecticut Community College for an award which allowed me to complete a residency in Mexico. Many, many thanks go to Peter Conners for his expertise and his patience with me, to Sandy Knight for the book design, and to all of the staff at BOA Editions for their fine work and close attention. Thanks also to Duc Tinh for his input on design, and to SL, who has offered to take up position as would-be Muse, but demands acknowledgment. Here it is: thank you! My gratitude extends as well to members of the Limerock Writers Salon, where many of these stories first emerged. Finally, thanks are due to Rilla Askew, Jonathan Baumbach, Peter Bricklebank, Shira Dentz, Richard O'Connor, Heath Prentis, Nava Renek, Donna Sefanisko: for all that you are and all that you do.

About the Author

Jessica Treat grew up in New England and lived for a number of years in Mexico City. She is the author of two previous story collections: *A Robber in the House* and *Not a Chance.* Her stories have been published in numerous anthologies and journals, including *Ms. Magazine, Epoch, Black Warrior Review, American Literary Review, Quarterly West,* and *Double Room.* She has received artist residency awards from Civitella Ranieri Foundation in Italy, Fundación Valparaíso in Spain, and an Artist Fellowship Award in fiction from the Connecticut Commission on the Arts. Jessica Treat is Professor of English at Northwestern Connecticut Community College where she coordinates the Mad River Literary Festival. She has read and presented her work at numerous festivals, literary venues and universities, including Brown University, New York University, Universidad de Almería (Spain), Boston Fiction Festival, and The Poetry Project. She lives with her son in a small town in the Berkshires.

BOA Editions, Ltd.
American Reader Series

No. 1   *Christmas at the Four Corners of the Earth*
         Prose by Blaise Cendrars
         Translated by Bertrand Mathieu

No. 2   *Pig Notes & Dumb Music: Prose on Poetry*
         By William Heyen

No. 3   *After-Images: Autobiographical Sketches*
         By W. D. Snodgrass

No. 4   *Walking Light: Memoirs and Essays on Poetry*
         By Stephen Dunn

No. 5   *To Sound Like Yourself: Essays on Poetry*
         By W. D. Snodgrass

No. 6   *You Alone Are Real to Me: Remembering Rainer
         Maria Rilke*
         By Lou Andreas-Salomé

No. 7   *Breaking the Alabaster Jar: Conversations with
         Li-Young Lee*
         Edited by Earl G. Ingersoll

No. 8   *I Carry A Hammer In My Pocket For Occasions
         Such As These*
         By Anthony Tognazzini

No. 9   *Unlucky Lucky Days*
         By Daniel Grandbois